HER HOLIDAY
RANCHER

NEW YORK TIMES BESTSELLING AUTHOR

CATHY McDAVID

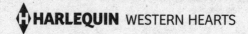

HARLEQUIN WESTERN HEARTS

Recycling programs
for this product may
not exist in your area.

HARLEQUIN® WESTERN HEARTS

ISBN-13: 978-1-335-50805-8

Her Holiday Rancher
First published in 2015.
This edition published in 2020.
Copyright © 2015 by Cathy McDavid

This edition published by arrangement with Harlequin Books S.A.

For questions and comments about the quality of this book,
please contact us at CustomerService@Harlequin.com.

Harlequin Enterprises ULC
22 Adelaide St. West, 40th Floor
Toronto, Ontario M5H 4E3, Canada
www.Harlequin.com

Printed in U.S.A.

Since 2006, *New York Times* bestselling author **Cathy McDavid** has been happily penning contemporary Westerns for Harlequin. Every day, she gets to write about handsome cowboys riding the range or busting a bronc. It's a tough job, but she's willing to make the sacrifice. Cathy shares her Arizona home with her own real-life sweetheart and a trio of odd pets. Her grown twins have left to embark on lives of their own, and she couldn't be prouder of their accomplishments.

To the two groups who have made me a better writer, given me guidance and unconditional support, and opened up a whole new world for me: my critique group (twelve years strong, can you believe it?) and Valley of the Sun Romance Writers. You are more than my friends, you are pieces of my heart.

Chapter 1

What the small brown mare lacked in size, she more than made up for in muscle and determination. Lowering her head, she put all her weight into her forequarters and plowed up the mountainside. With each powerful step, dirt and small rocks exploded from beneath her hooves, tumbling downward like a miniature landslide.

Gabriel Dempsey rode the mare hard to the top of the rise. Once there, they stopped to rest, both of them breathing hard, their legs trembling. Despite her exertion, the mare would keep going if he asked. She wasn't just young and strong. The blood from generations of wild mustangs ran in her veins, infusing her with a spirit and unbreakable will unmatched by any other breed of horse.

No, it was Gabe who couldn't go on. He was spent. Utterly and completely exhausted. Not from the trail ride, but from the emotional events of the past four days.

Exactly seventeen months and twenty-three days after the doctor's initial prognosis, cancer had taken his father's life.

Today, the family had memorialized him in a service that had brought out half the town of Mustang Valley, along with a hundred other mourners from all over Arizona. Tomorrow Gabe and his family would spread August Dempsey's ashes in the flower garden behind the house.

His father would spend eternity where he, Gabe's grandfather and great-grandfather had lived and toiled their entire lives, on the three-thousand-acre Dos Estrellas Ranch.

Shading his eyes against the glaring afternoon sun, Gabe stared at the ranch nestled in the valley below. From this distance, the house, barns and outbuildings appeared deceptively small, like a painting hanging on a wall. Adding to the illusion were horses in the back pastures and sixteen hundred head of cattle dotting the extensive grazing lands beyond the pastures.

Grief suddenly gripped Gabe's chest like a giant metal vise, colder than the November wind ripping across the rise from the slopes of the nearby McDowell Mountains.

He sat straight in the saddle, refusing to succumb to emotion or show the slightest sign of weakness. Even out here, where there wasn't another living soul for two miles in any direction. The battle facing him at home promised to be a difficult one. This was only the beginning.

Among all the mourners gathered at the ranch to pay their final respects to one of Mustang Valley's greatest citizens were two strangers. Gabe's half brothers. August Dempsey's *legitimate* sons. Rumor had it, they'd come to claim their share of the Dos Estrellas Ranch, left to them by the father they barely knew. Gabe would know for sure tomorrow afternoon at the reading of the will.

If they did inherit, he intended to fight them tooth and nail, regardless if he had a legal right to the ranch or not. He was the son who'd worked side by side with their father for over two decades. The son who was proud of his heritage and treasured it. Who loved the ranch with the same fervor and devotion as any Dempsey before him. He hadn't left as a kid and never returned.

Giving the mare a nudge, Gabe followed the narrow deer trail south as it alternately dipped, climbed and snaked. Not far below him, a line of barbed wire fencing ran parallel to the trail.

The fence separated Dos Estrellas from its nearest neighbor and longtime cattle-ranching rival, the Small Change, though *small* was a misnomer. The ranch was twice the size of Dos Estrellas and these days, owner Theo McGraw ran close to thirty-five hundred head of fat, sassy cattle.

Cancer was a greedy disease and had taken more than Gabe's father. Astronomical medical bills continued to pour in daily, many of which weren't covered by health insurance. With no choice, Gabe and his mother had sold off what they could, depleting Dos Estrellas's resources. It wasn't enough, and the wolves continued to prowl outside their door. Gabe and his half brothers might well wind up fighting over a pile of scraps.

The trail abruptly veered west. Gabe and the mare dropped down into the mouth of a ravine thick with creosote, sage and cacti.

Last month's heavy rains had resulted in abundant desert foliage that had survived the recent cold snap and remained a vibrant green.

At the bottom of the ravine, the mare halted. Lifting her head, she smelled the air, her ears pricked forward.

"What do you see, Bonita?"

Gabe had been raised around horses and trusted their instincts, especially those of a mustang born in the wild. Something was amiss.

He sat still and listened, his eyes scanning the uneven horizon. Coyotes and bobcats regularly traveled this ravine, along with the occasional mountain lion. None were an immediate threat. Desert predators usually avoided humans. The mare's survival instincts, however, were powerful, and she might attempt to flee.

She didn't, which Gabe found interesting. Whatever lurked in the bush clearly wasn't a predator. What, then—

A sharp, shrill screech pierced the air followed by a faint cry of distress. Pausing long enough to choose the best course, he set off in the direction of the sounds, taking the steep trail at a brisk trot, the fastest he dare go without endangering himself or Bonita.

At the top of the rise, his heart stopped cold. The entire back half of a horse was submerged in a sinkhole, nearly up to the saddle horn. The horse's head and front legs stuck out of the narrow opening at a painful and impossible angle, almost as if he were standing up. Covered with mud and wide-eyed with fright, the horse flailed helplessly.

On the ground in front of the horse, beyond the reach of the sinkhole, a woman attempted to free him by jerking on the reins and calling out encouragements. Both woman and horse were clearly done in from the struggle. Without help, the horse would eventually die. Every moment counted.

Gabe dug his boot heels into Bonita's sides. The mare didn't hesitate and carried them down the steep slope. More than once she nearly lost her footing, slipping and sliding over the rocky terrain. At the bottom, Gabe tugged hard on the reins, slowing Bonita and bringing her under control.

"Are you okay?" he called to the woman, covering the remaining distance at a lope.

"I need help." She spared him the briefest

of glances, paused for a fraction of a second, then went right back to pulling on the reins.

Gabe's brain registered two things simultaneously. First, there was no way in hell she was ever going to save that horse by herself. Maybe no one could. Second, he'd seen the woman a mere four hours earlier at the funeral. She'd sat in the rear pew of the crowded church next to her father, Theo McGraw, Gabe's father's rival.

"Hang on." Gabe jumped off Bonita and, leading the mare, approached Reese McGraw. "Got yourself in a fix here."

"I missed the hole. It was covered with twigs and dead leaves."

Sinkholes weren't uncommon in the desert, especially after heavy rains, though they were generally larger. This particular hazard was deceptively small, measuring three and a half feet at its widest point, and easy to miss.

"It happens," he said matter-of-factly.

"Can you help me get him out?"

"I'll try."

She swallowed, and Gabe noticed the dried streaks on her cheeks. Had she been crying or was the cold wind responsible for her tears?

"Are you hurt?"

"No." She shook her head, and a hank of

shoulder-length strawberry blond hair loosened from its clip. As if sensing his gaze, she said, "I lost my hat when I bailed off."

"We'll find it later." The hat didn't matter. He was simply trying to calm her. She'd need all her strength for the ordeal ahead, along with her concentration.

She continued tugging on the reins, which the confused horse fought, jerking his big head to the side rather than using the added momentum to hoist himself out of the hole.

"Take it easy," Gabe said.

"I can't. If I do, he'll sink deeper."

"No, he won't. Trust me." Gabe put up a restraining hand. "Hold steady, but don't pull. Not yet. Wait until I tell you to."

"What are you going to do?" Worry filled her eyes.

Gabe hadn't noticed their vibrant green color before. Then again, he generally avoided Reese. "Well, if we can't drag him out, I'll ride for help."

Neither of them voiced aloud what they were doubtless thinking; there may not be time for that. Who knew the depth of the hole? One wrong move, and the horse's own weight could drag him under the mud.

Gabe decided he'd seen enough death for

one week. If it was at all humanly possible, he would save this horse.

"Focus on keeping his head up," he told Reese.

Gabe lined up Bonita next to her. The mare obediently stood quiet. Next, he removed the coil of rope from his saddlebag and fastened one end to a metal ring on the right side of his saddle. Letting out rope a foot at a time, he neared the panicked horse.

"Easy now, partner," he cooed. "That's right."

Sides heaving and nostrils flaring, the big paint stared at Gabe. Perhaps his imagination was working overtime, but he swore the horse understood he was trying to help.

He continued talking to the paint as he pondered how best to fasten the rope. Simply around the head wouldn't provide enough leverage. They'd strangle the horse before they rescued him. No way could he feed the rope beneath the horse's chest and behind his front legs, which would be ideal. He'd likely injure his hand in the process.

Gabe decided to run the rope through the girth on either side of the saddle. A tricky operation. One miscalculation and the results could end in disaster. For the horse and Gabe.

"Here goes nothing."

Thankfully, the horse remained quiet while Gabe circled him and attached the rope to both sides, looping it behind the saddle horn for added resistance. It was the best he could do under the circumstances. By the time he finished, sweat had gathered on his forehead and soaked the inside of his shirt.

He removed his cowboy hat and combed his fingers through his damp hair.

"You holding up?" he asked Reese.

"I'm fine."

Right. She looked ready to drop. He gave her credit, though. She wasn't a quitter.

"Then, let's get this horse out."

He patted Bonita's rump. She'd done well so far. What came next would be the real test.

Glancing over his shoulder, he inspected his handiwork one last time. The big paint cooperated by not moving. That, or he was past the point of fighting.

Gabe stood at Bonita's head and gripped the side of her bridle above the bit. The rope stretched taut from both sides of her saddle to both sides of the paint's.

"Good girl." He rubbed her soft nose. "You can do it."

Bonita nuzzled his hands, not the least bit concerned.

He peered over her back at Reese. "You ready?"

"Yes." She didn't look it. Her hands shook and her face was alarmingly pale.

"Your job is to keep that horse's head up. Bonita and I will do the rest. You understand?"

"Got it."

"Any sign of trouble, you let go. I mean it. Don't put any of us in danger."

She nodded.

"All right then. On the count of three. One, two, three." He clucked to Bonita and yanked on her bridle.

Muscles straining, hide quivering, the mare took one step forward, then a second.

Gabe glanced back at the paint. He'd yet to move, other than stretching his head and neck out as far as they would go.

"Come on, boy. Now or never."

They could only do so much. It was entirely up to the horse. If he didn't haul himself out of the sinkhole and onto solid ground, he would die right where he was.

Bonita didn't quit and, once again, Gabe admired the little mare he'd handpicked from his friend Cara's herd of rehabilitated wild mustangs.

"He's doing it!" Reese hollered.

Gabe looked. True enough, the horse had found the will to save itself. With tremendous effort, he dug his front hooves into the ground and, with the aid of the primitive pulley, climbed out of the deep mud.

"Don't quit on us now." Gabe wasn't sure who he was talking to. The horse or Bonita or Reese. Did it really matter?

With a final mighty groan, the horse heaved himself out, landing with a grunt on his belly. Gabe let go of Bonita and rushed to the paint, afraid the unsteady horse would slide back into the hole.

One rope in each hand, he pulled with every ounce of his strength. It wasn't enough.

"Help me," he said to Reese.

In a flash, she was there.

"Grab the saddle."

She did, and by some miracle, they dragged the horse two feet before they gave out. The ground beneath the heavy horse held. He lay there, his back legs suspended over the hole and dripping mud, his breathing coming in great gusts.

"Give him a few minutes," Gabe said, flexing his cramped and aching fingers. "Then we'll get him up."

"Okay." Reese stood bent at the waist, her hands braced on her knees.

Gabe, too, rested. How long had this taken? Thirty minutes? An hour? He wasn't sure. Except that, for whatever time it took, he hadn't once thought of his father's death.

"My God, Gabe, you did it! You saved him."

The next instant, Reese slammed into him, her arms circling his neck. He automatically steadied them both by holding on to her.

"Thank you," she said, clinging to him, her face buried in his coat.

He stared at the top of her head, momentarily stunned. He'd touched Reese just one other time in their entire lives. They'd been in high school, at their senior prom. He'd cradled her while she cried and begged him not to tell anyone she was pregnant.

"You should call the vet right away."

Reese didn't need Gabe to tell her that. Of course she'd call the vet. The second she and General arrived home. But, seeing as Gabe had rescued her father's favorite horse, and she was eternally grateful, she bit her tongue.

"I will."

They'd finally managed to coax General to

his feet after a ten-minute respite. The poor gelding was utterly depleted and stood with his head hanging low and his nose to the ground. If it were at all possible to drive a truck and trailer into these rugged hills, she'd do it. Unfortunately, she and General would have to travel by foot.

"Come on." Gabe grabbed hold of his mare's reins and mounted with the grace and ease of someone who rode daily. Once seated, he stared at her expectantly.

"What?" she asked.

He patted the mare's hindquarters. "Climb aboard. Daylight's wasting."

Reese blinked in astonishment. "You're suggesting we ride double?"

"Your horse won't make it thirty feet carrying you."

Did he believe her a nitwit? Just because she'd been away from Mustang Valley for a long time didn't mean she'd forgotten everything she'd ever learned.

"I was planning on walking." She picked her hat off the ground from where it had fallen. "At least to the road."

"I'll take you," he said, as if it were already decided. He removed his left foot from the stirrup.

"You don't have to do this."

"You're tuckered out. And it'll be dark soon."

He was right. The sun had started dropping, along with the temperature. General was wet and starting to shake. If she didn't get him moving soon, he'd catch a chill. Her, too.

"Fine."

He raised one brow as if to remark, "Funny way of saying thanks."

Gabe had always been able to convey enormous emotion using very few words. It was a quality she'd found intriguing from the time they were young. That, and his good looks. His Hispanic heritage, courtesy of his mother, blended beautifully with his Dempsey genes. Dark hair, silver-gray eyes, a strong jaw, tanned complexion and a wide mouth created for kissing.

Not that she had kissed him. Or even thought about it. Okay, not much.

She and Gabe had grown up neighbors, but also rivals, thanks to their fathers' lifelong feud. They'd steered as clear of each other as much as humanly possible in a small community the size of Mustang Valley.

Six months ago, she'd returned after a twelve-year absence. This afternoon was the first time she and Gabe had spoken since the night of their senior prom.

She should, she supposed, thank him for something else besides saving General. He'd kept his promise and said nothing about her pregnancy. If he had, she would have heard. Secrets like hers were too titillating to resist repeating.

Holding General's reins with her right hand, she clasped Gabe's outstretched one with her left. Then, putting her foot in the empty stirrup, she let him assist her onto the mare's back.

"Can she carry the two of us?" she asked, settling in behind Gabe. The mare was on the small side and worn out after her recent efforts.

"She'll manage."

The next moment, they were off. At the mare's first hop over a hole, Reese grabbed Gabe's middle rather than be dumped on the ground. She swore he chuckled beneath his breath. Or it might have been the wind.

"How's he doing?" Gabe asked after a few minutes.

Reese looked behind her at General, and her heart hurt. "He's limping on his right rear leg."

"Will he make it to the road?"

"I think so." Then she could call the house and have someone from the Small Change meet them with a truck and trailer.

If her phone had worked when General fell into the sinkhole, she wouldn't have had to rely on Gabe's help. She'd tried repeatedly to get a signal, but there had been none. She was lucky he'd ridden by. And that it was today rather than tomorrow, after the reading of August Dempsey's will.

"Thank you again," she said. "I owe you."

He simply grunted.

"For a lot more than saving General," she added, wondering if he understood her meaning.

"I'm a man of my word."

Okay, he did understand. "For which I'm very appreciative."

She waited for him to ask her what had happened to the baby. Where she'd gone when she left Mustang Valley. What she'd done. If she'd ever told Blake Nolan, the baby's father.

Gabe remained stoically silent, and she sensed an unmistakable tension coursing through him.

The next mile passed slowly. Every few minutes, Reese checked on General. His limp was getting worse, and she gritted her teeth. How far to the road? She craned her neck in order to look ahead over Gabe's broad shoulder.

In hindsight, she should have waited to take General out until later in the week when she was less busy. But she hated seeing the stout gelding cooped up day after day in his stall, barely ridden.

It wasn't her father's fault. He would exercise General every day if his health permitted. This morning, simply crawling out of bed to attend August Dempsey's funeral had been a challenge. Riding was out of the question.

"It was nice of you to come today," Gabe said, rousing her from her thoughts.

"My father may not have gotten along with yours, but he respected him greatly. We wouldn't have missed the funeral."

Gabe's response was another noncommittal grunt.

The mare stumbled on the steep incline, causing Reese to grip Gabe's waist tighter.

"Maybe I should get off and walk," she suggested, acutely aware of his broad, strong back through the thick fabric of his coat.

"We're almost to the road."

It was the longest fifteen minutes ever. Immediately upon dismounting, she examined General. The poor horse was on the verge of collapsing.

She got on her cell phone, and breathed a sigh of relief when her call connected.

"Hi, Dad." She summarized the situation, including how Gabe had rescued her and General.

"I'm glad you're all right and that Gabe was riding by." Relief filled his voice. "He's a good man."

Reese knew her father's praise was sincere. The rivalry between him and August Dempsey was strictly over business and had nothing to do with character. In another lifetime, under different circumstances, the two might have been friends.

"I'll tell him myself when I see him," her father continued.

"No, Dad. You've had a long day." She turned away from Gabe, who still sat astride the mare, and said in a low voice, "You need your rest. Send Enrico."

"He'll drive, but I'm damn well going with him."

It was the best she could hope for. Her father was a stubborn old fool when he set his mind to something. Like not telling anyone about his Parkinson's. How long could he realistically expect to keep hiding his disease? He was starting to show symptoms, and people were becoming suspicious. Like Enrico, who'd worked for the McGraws since before Reese had left.

"Fine." What choice did she have, short of telling Enrico? And her father would never forgive her for that. He was a proud man. "See you when you get here."

"Be careful, honey."

Reese glanced at Gabe, then chided herself. Of course, her father was referring to General. She had nothing to worry about from Gabe, who was scrutinizing her every move with those compelling eyes of his.

She said goodbye and disconnected the call. Returning to the weary horse, she gave his neck a loving stroke.

Eying Gabe, she said, "You'd better hurry if you want to get home before dark."

"I'll wait until your ride gets here."

"It could be a while."

Truthfully, she had no idea how long her father and Enrico would be. She was simply providing Gabe with an excuse to leave.

"I have time."

"Aren't you hungry?"

He shrugged one shoulder. "The house is filled with food."

She could well imagine. As expected, friends and family had stopped by, dropping off casseroles, covered dishes and baked goods as they paid their respects. Food and funerals seemed to go together.

"Are you?" Gabe asked. "Hungry?"

"A little." Between the service this morning, caring for her father and worrying about tomorrow's reading of the will, she'd missed lunch.

Riding General hadn't been solely to exercise the barn-bound horse. She'd needed a mental vacation in the worst way.

"Mostly I'm cold," she added.

Gabe dismounted, unbuckled the saddlebag and reached inside. A moment later, he produced a yellow rain poncho and a small, rectangular object she couldn't quite make out.

"Here." He approached her, his stride confident and, she had to admit, sexy.

A small thrill wound through her. She blamed the stressful events of the day. It couldn't possibly be attraction. To Gabe Dempsey? No way.

"Here." He shook out the rain poncho, removed her hat and placed the poncho over her head.

"I don't need—"

"Shut up, Reese." He replaced her hat and fastened the top snap on the poncho, the one beneath her chin. "It'll help keep you warm."

The thrill turned into a flush as his fingers brushed her exposed skin. Who needed a poncho when Gabe's proximity was enough to warm her from the inside?

"O…kay." Please don't let him notice the effect he was having on her.

"Here." He lifted her hand and pressed the object he'd taken from the saddlebag into it. "Enjoy."

She stared at the energy bar. "I can't."

"Why not?"

"Because…"

"You're as stubborn as your father." A smile touched his lips.

She thought it might be his first one in days or even weeks. Nothing could be worse than losing a loved one.

"I'll eat this," she said, "but only if we share."

"You drive a hard bargain, Miss McGraw."

He hadn't seen anything yet. Just wait until they butted heads over his father's estate.

Ripping open the wrapper, she removed the energy bar and broke it in half.

He accepted the piece, his fingers brushing hers. Was it intentional? She wouldn't put it past him. Gabe had always been a ladies' man, starting in high school. She was surprised he'd reached the age of thirty without some woman snapping him up.

Then again, no one had snapped up Reese, either, though she'd come close once. Perhaps Gabe was like her, married to his work.

They didn't speak while they ate. Reese stared up the road. No sign of her father yet. When she was done with her half of the energy bar, she checked again on General, then returned to Gabe, pulling the poncho closer around her.

"Still cold?" Gabe asked.

"A little."

"We could huddle for warmth."

Her eyes widened. "You're kidding."

His smile returned. "I don't bite, Reese."

Sweet heaven, he was gorgeous. "I'm fine." She was not letting Gabe touch her, much less hold her.

Headlights appeared in the distance, about a mile up the road. Reese released a long sigh. As assistant manager of Southern Arizona

Bank, it was her job, her duty, to conduct herself professionally and impersonally with the Dempsey family. Huddling with Gabe, even for warmth in extreme weather conditions, wasn't either of those things.

She waved as the truck and trailer neared. "Dad's here. You don't have to stay."

"All right," he said, his tone unreadable, and mounted the mare.

"What about your poncho?"

"Keep it." Gabe tugged on the brim of his cowboy hat. "See you around."

She watched him ride off into the darkness toward Dos Estrellas, barely noticing the truck rumble to a stop behind her.

He'd do more than see her around. Thanks to August Dempsey revising his will six months ago, Reese was about to become a fixture in the Dempsey brothers' lives, and there was nothing they could do to change it.

Chapter 2

"If you'll all please have a seat, we can get started." Hector Fuentes made a sweeping gesture that included everyone in the spacious living room. He lowered himself onto the cowhide upholstered recliner where Gabe's father had once dozed every afternoon while waiting for Raquel Salazar, Gabe's mother, to finish putting supper on the table.

Better it was the family attorney occupying his father's favorite chair than one of his half brothers, Gabe thought sourly.

Brothers. The word still sounded strange to him. Two full days in their company had made no difference. Neither had attending the funeral together yesterday or sharing coffee with them before spreading their father's ashes in the flower garden this morning. Gabe didn't know these men.

It was his mother's idea they take the guest suite in the house rather than stay at the Wild Horse Bed and Breakfast in town. "They're family," she'd told Gabe. "Your father would have wanted it. And we have plenty of room."

Gabe had seethed in silence instead of arguing. Did his mother have to be so nice to them? If they inherited the ranch, she'd be thrown out of her home.

After casting tentative glances at each other, the brothers in question sat in matching wingback chairs—which happened to be directly opposite Gabe, his mother and Cara Alvarez. Cara was the daughter of Raquel's childhood friend Leena and had lived with Gabe's family the past two years.

Consciously or subconsciously, Gabe, Raquel and Cara had made a united front on the couch.

No one else had been invited to the reading of the will, giving Gabe reason to believe those present were the only ones named as beneficiaries.

He swallowed, but the knot of pain residing above his heart didn't loosen. Those two men shouldn't be here. His father had promised Gabe the ranch. Many times over.

What had changed August Dempsey's mind at the eleventh hour? Was the cancer to blame? Had all the medications and treatments ravaged his body and mind? Or had he lied to Gabe and intended to give the ranch to his legitimate sons all along, leaving Gabe with nothing?

Using his briefcase as a lap desk, Hector Fuentes cleared his throat and tapped a thin stack of papers into a perfect rectangle. "If it's all right with everyone, I'll skip the standard legalese and get right to the bequests. I've brought copies of the entire will for everyone and will distribute them later to those who want one."

Gabe wanted a copy. He'd bet his brothers would, too.

Hector smiled at Cara before beginning. "To Cara Alvarez, who has been like a daughter to Raquel and myself, I grant exclusive use of five hundred acres of Dos Estrellas pasture land, to include parcels six, seven and eight, for her mustang sanctuary."

Cara's hand flew to her mouth, and she inhaled sharply. The sanctuary and its horses meant a great deal to her. For his father to include her in his will showed how much he'd considered her to be part of the family.

His mother bit back a sob and placed an arm around Cara's shoulders.

"Cara is to have use of the parcels for as long as she wants," Hector continued, "or for as long as Dos Estrellas remains in the family."

Remains in the family. The words gave Gabe hope. His father wouldn't have allowed Cara exclusive use of nearly one-sixth of the ranch and not bequeath Gabe the entirety of it. Nothing else made sense.

Hector continued, outlining the specifics. "Do you have any questions?" he asked Cara when he was done.

She shook her head, tears filling her eyes.

"Raquel, the love of my life, and Cara both," Hector said, "will continue to reside at Dos Estrellas and occupy the ranch house for as long as they choose or for as long as the ranch remains in the family."

Again, Cara inhaled sharply and his mother softly sobbed. Gabe, on the other hand, began to worry. What was with the wording, *as long as the ranch remains in the family*? Twice his father had used it. There must be some significance.

"Any questions?" Hector repeated when he'd finished with the specifics.

"No," Gabe's mother and Cara replied simultaneously.

Hector then listed smaller bequests. Gabe's mother was to receive ownership of August's favorite dog. She, along with Gabe and a close cousin, were to get his jewelry, personal items and cherished mementos.

Gabe studied his brothers' faces during the reading. He wouldn't recognize either of them as being related to him or their father. Other than the fact they all three stood over six feet tall, there were no noticeable physical similarities. With their blond hair and blue eyes, Josh, the oldest brother, and Cole must resemble their mother.

Neither did they look like the boys he remembered from his childhood. Gabe had been in first grade, Josh second and Cole in kindergarten when an older child on the playground had pointed to the brothers and told Gabe in a taunting voice that they were his father's *real* sons. The boy had then called Gabe's mother a name he hadn't understood at the time, but instinctively knew was the worst of insults.

Angry and hurt and experiencing feelings

he couldn't explain, much less process, Gabe had passed the rest of the day in a blur. Arriving home after school, he'd gone straight from the bus to his mother and told her about what the boy had said, omitting the bad name.

She'd hugged him, smoothed his hair and insisted he forget about it. Gabe might have, except the same thing happened two days later. Instead of retaliating against the boy, Gabe went after Josh, who was both older and bigger than him. The attack, poorly executed, nonetheless cost him three days' suspension from school for fighting.

His mother had been furious with him. She'd also been saddened. It was the first Gabe had learned that his father, who visited once or twice a week in the evenings, had a wife and children living on a ranch outside of Mustang Valley. It took Gabe several years to fully understand his family's unusual dynamics, long after he and his mother had moved to Dos Estrellas.

Did Josh remember the school tussle? Did he know it was Gabe who had hit him and what had made him so angry? Probably not. At least, his face gave no indication.

"Last, is my beloved Dos Estrellas Ranch,

which has been in the Dempsey family for three generations."

Hector's voice jarred Gabe from his thoughts. Every muscle in his body tightened. He willed himself not to look at his brothers, but at Hector instead. They would not see how important this moment was to him, or his devastation if the rumors turned out to be true and Gabe lost the ranch.

Beside him, his mother shifted and murmured under her breath. Cara grabbed his hand and squeezed.

"I leave the ranch equally to my three sons, Josh, Cole and Gabe."

Pain sliced through Gabe, leaving him numb. He hadn't inherited the ranch. Worse, his father had named him third after his two legitimate sons, whom he hadn't seen in twenty-four years.

Betrayal. It was the emotion Gabe hadn't been able to define when he was six. It was also the emotion that gripped him now, fresh as the day on the playground with Josh.

"See, I told you, *mijo*," his mother said in a whisper, "your father did not forget you."

Not forget him? He might as well have. Gabe was supposed to share ownership of Dos Estrellas? With them?

"He promised to leave the ranch to Gabe," Cara hissed.

"Hush," his mother ordered.

"It's not fair." Cara's voice rose, loud enough to draw the stares of everyone in the room. "Gabe's worked the land. He knows the cattle business and how the ranch is run." She gestured to Josh and Cole. "They don't have the first clue. They're rodeo competitors, for crying out loud."

"We can hear you," Josh said.

Cole grunted and stared angrily out the large bay window.

Gabe fumed. What was the guy's problem? He had nothing to be angry about.

"If we could please continue," Hector scolded in an attempt to bring the reading back under control.

Cara didn't apologize. She didn't say anything, merely folded her arms across her middle.

With a warning nod in her direction, Hector carried on, reading August's words. "My good attorney has advised me to cover the many details on a separate page. I've done that, merely to satisfy him, mind you." A hint of amusement flashed in Hector's eyes. "But, in a nutshell, Dos Estrellas can't be sold in its entirety unless all three of my sons are in agreement. And while individual shares can be sold, it is my fervent wish my beloved ranch remains in the family for many future generations, and the grandchildren I didn't live long enough to see will grow up here, fine, strong and healthy like my own boys."

Gabe almost choked. Was his father serious? The two men sitting across from him hadn't grown up at the ranch. As children they'd moved six hundred miles away to Northern California and never once come back, ignoring the requests to visit their dying father and say goodbye.

He half listened to the rest of the reading. Violet Hathaway, the ranch's livestock manager, along with the Dempsey housekeeper of twenty-plus years, were to retain their jobs. Lastly, there was a mention of selling shares to one another and how the profits were to be distributed.

Profits, right. What a joke. There weren't any, and hadn't been since August had become ill.

"Questions?" Hector asked, sounding a lot like a parrot.

Gabe shook his head. He would read his copy of the will later, when he was less agitated and better able to focus, though it wouldn't make much difference.

The empty hole inside him ached. He'd admired, respected and loved his father with boundless devotion. Now he feared he might have been wrong. Whether his father had realized it or not, he'd forced Gabe into partnership with his brothers and, by the looks on their faces, they were as unhappy about the outcome as Gabe.

"Are we done?" Cole asked, his tone sharp.

"Not quite." Hector set his briefcase on the floor by his feet. "There's the matter of the trustee."

"Trustee?" Gabe's mother leaned forward. "What is a trustee?"

"The Dos Estrellas and August's other property are actually held in the trust he established. As with all trusts, a person or entity is designated to oversee the trust and carry out the terms of the will according to the decedent's wishes. Typically, the trustee makes the distributions, and, in this case, will oversee the management of the estate per August's instructions."

"Dad hired a manager?" Gabe couldn't believe his ears.

"Not exactly. You and your brothers will

run the ranch. But's the trustee's job to make sure you're running it according to the terms of your father's will. For instance, your mother and Cara continue to live here as long as they choose and Cara's mustang sanctuary is protected."

That sounded reasonable, Gabe supposed.

"You should know your father gave the trustee full financial powers until the ranch operates in the black for at least one full year, and all his medical bills are paid off. The trustee's duties will end only then or if the ranch is sold."

"I don't understand," Josh said.

"Essentially, while you and your brothers run the ranch, the trustee will be pulling the purse strings."

If Gabe wasn't already in a state of shock, this latest bombshell would have knocked him to his knees. His father had preferred for someone outside the family handle the ranch's finances over his son? His sons?

"Who's the trustee?" Gabe asked.

Hector waited a beat before responding. "The Southern Arizona Bank."

Mustang Valley's sole financial institution. Gabe was familiar with them, like everyone else in the community.

"Why?"

"A trustee is supposed to abide by the terms of the will." Hector shrugged. "Unfortunately, they don't always. It can happen when family members are put in charge. Emotions run high. As a result, some individuals choose an entity, such as a bank, or an attorney, to act as trustee. They tend to adhere more strictly to the terms of the will and keep emotions out of it."

Perhaps Gabe's father had the foresight to realize forcing his three sons into an unwanted partnership would guarantee high-running emotions.

The front doorbell rang, startling several of the room's occupants. Not Hector. He made his way to the large, ornately carved wooden door.

"Who could that be?" Gabe's mother moved as if to rise. "I specifically requested no visitors this afternoon."

"It's all right," Hector said. "I arranged for the representative from the bank to be here today in order to meet you all and put your fears to rest."

He opened the heavy door. It swung wide, revealing a feminine silhouette cast in dark shadows from the sun's slanting rays.

"Am I early?" the woman asked.

"Not at all, come in," he said. "We're ready for you."

Gabe blinked as the representative stepped across the threshold, convinced he was seeing things. It couldn't be. This had to be a mistake. Or someone's idea of a sick joke. He wasn't sure if he should shout in protest or laugh out loud.

Hector took the young, professionally dressed woman by the arm and led her to the center of the room as if she were on display.

"For those of you who haven't met her before, this is Reese McGraw, assistant manager at Southern Arizona Bank and the trustee of August Dempsey's estate."

"Thank you." Reese accepted the cup of coffee Raquel Salazar offered and smiled in appreciation. Other than the attorney Hector Fuentes, Gabe's mother was the only one to show Reese any friendliness so far.

It was to be expected. Even under normal circumstances, no one in the Dempsey or Salazar families would be pleased to welcome her, the daughter of Theo McGraw. To learn she was the employee at Southern Arizona Bank in charge of overseeing August Dempsey's estate, well, it must be a shock.

Gabe's features hardened each time he glanced at her, which was often. If he was trying to scare her off, it wouldn't work. Reese was here to stay.

It was, she mused, a far cry from the way he'd looked at her yesterday while waiting for her father and Enrico to arrive with the truck and trailer. When he'd buttoned her into the rain poncho, she swore the heat of attraction had flared in his eyes. Not to mention his touch lingered far longer than necessary.

The poncho had kept her warm, all right. That, and the effects of his proximity.

Reese silently scolded herself, alarmed by the direction of her thoughts. She'd known Gabe most of her life, but not once entertained any romantic notions about him. What had changed since their last conversation twelve years ago? Was it her or him?

"You are welcome," Raquel said in her lilting Hispanic accent. "How is your father doing? He looked a little pale yesterday at the service."

Reese gave a small start. Raquel had noticed her father's appearance? Surely, she'd had much, much more on her mind at the funeral than Theo McGraw. Reese swallowed. Soon, her father's symptoms would become increasingly apparent. Hiding his Parkinson's would be impossible.

Good. His constant care, and the tremendous burden that came with it, were taking a toll on her, physically and emotionally. He needed help managing his symptoms beyond her limited abilities. Yet he refused to hire an experienced health care professional, convinced people in Mustang Valley would view him differently. Think less of him.

She wished he could see how wrong he was. The same people he feared would pity him had rallied to comfort the family and offer support during August Dempsey's long illness. They would do the same for her father.

She blamed the damnable McGraw pride, which her father possessed in abundance. She, too, perhaps. Hadn't she left town shortly after realizing she was pregnant with Blake Nolan's baby, convinced people would talk behind her and her father's backs?

"He was tired," she explained to Raquel. "His arthritis has been keeping him awake at night."

Her hostess sighed expansively. "I understand. I have my own complaints. Give him my regards, will you?"

"Of course."

She patted Reese's arm before gliding away.

Reese admired Gabe's mother. While the sadness in Raquel's eyes showed evidence of her grief and sorrow, she remained strong and stalwart. Perhaps, in a way, she was relieved at his passing. August had been in considerable pain at the end, and no one wanted to see their loved one needlessly suffer.

Funny they'd never married. August and his wife divorced twenty-plus years ago. Reese was curious. Reading the entirety of his will hadn't provided any insight.

Sipping her coffee, she made her way to Cara Alvarez, who, by her estimation, was the one person with the least reason to dislike her. They had once been school friends, after all. Before the feud between August and Reese's father severed their budding friendship.

"Hey, how you doing?"

Cara glanced up from the spot on the floor she'd been staring at. "All right."

"I'm sorry for your loss."

"Thank you."

With her luxurious black hair and striking beauty, Cara might have been related to Raquel and not just the daughter she never had. One prominent difference was their eyes. While Raquel's sparked with a wide array of emotions, Cara's alternated between listlessness and despair. They had been that way since the tragic death of her toddler son two years ago.

"I hear you're doing great things with the mustang sanctuary," Reese said.

"I don't know about great." Cara shifted and resumed staring, this time out the window.

Was she remembering her son's funeral?

Reese decided her former schoolmate wasn't in the mood for conversation. "If there's anything you need, feel free to call me or come by the bank."

"Okay."

She touched Cara's arm before crossing the room. Feeling a prickling on the back of her neck, she turned and found Gabe staring at her from a far corner of the room. He stood by himself. No surprise, anger radiated off him in waves.

Reese squared her shoulders, refusing to wilt beneath the visual assault. She was at the ranch in an official capacity. Gabe and his family may not like the fact she was the trustee, but there was nothing they could do about it. August Dempsey's last wishes would be honored.

Lifting her coffee cup in acknowledgment,

she nodded at Gabe. He responded with raised brows and a look of surprise. How about that? She'd bested him. Surely it was a first.

Pleased with herself, she continued her casual stroll of the room. Hector was currently immersed in conversation with Raquel. From what Reese could discern, he was answering the questions she'd have gladly done if asked.

She'd certainly chosen a rough road to travel, though she wouldn't have refused the assignment. Losing her credibility at the bank, and possibly her position, weren't options. She needed a job with decent income and one that enabled her to be close to her father. Assistant manager of Southern Arizona Bank fit the bill perfectly.

Besides, she liked her job. And, if she said so herself, she was good at it.

Finishing her coffee, she started for the kitchen, planning to dispose of her cup in the sink. At the large archway separating the dining room from the kitchen, she paused. The strains of what was clearly a private conversation reached her ears from the other side of the archway and around the corner. It was between Josh Dempsey and his brother Cole.

"What am I going to do with one-third of the ranch?" Cole demanded irritably. "I don't want it. I don't want anything that belonged to him."

"Let's get our copy of the will and read through it," Josh suggested. "The terms may not be ironclad."

"You heard what the attorney said."

Cole had understood correctly. The will was ironclad. August had been thorough, perhaps anticipating a conflict.

"Maybe we can contest it."

"And where are we going to find the money for that?" Cole scoffed. "Getting custody of your kids drained your bank account."

Reese recalled reading the background information Hector had provided on the Dempsey brothers. According to the report, Josh was locked in a bitter legal battle with his ex-wife over custody of their two young children.

"Take it easy, Cole. My financial problems aren't what's making you mad."

"You're right. I don't want to be here, and I'm sorry we came."

"Give it another day or two. We'll figure out a way to get your money."

"*Our* money, you mean. Don't forget, brother, you want your share as badly as I want mine. Attorneys aren't cheap."

Reese retreated, concerned by what she'd heard. Growing up in Mustang Valley, she knew about August's first family and that there was no love lost between him and his sons. But he must have wanted to make amends. Why else would he have modified his will six months ago? Obviously, his two sons didn't appreciate the gesture.

Should she tell Gabe? Was it her place? No, probably not. But nothing stopped her from dropping a hint or two about his brothers' intentions.

He hadn't left the corner. Seeing his hard expression, Reese had second thoughts. Perhaps she should speak to Hector instead. Though what could he do? The same as her, alert Gabe, who'd likely be more receptive to the family attorney than her.

She wavered, still debating and well aware she was drawing attention to herself. A moment later, she headed straight for Gabe.

He didn't so much as blink at her approach. The guy had nerves of steel.

"I wanted to thank you again for helping me yesterday," she said.

"How's the horse?"

"Fine. A bit sore, but otherwise unharmed. The vet prescribed pain relievers, an anti-inflammatory and a week's rest." She mentioned the vet's visit strictly to let Gabe know she wasn't lax when it came to the well-being of the McGraw horses.

"You were lucky."

"I was." She hoped he noted the sincerity she was trying to convey. "I can't imagine what I would have done if you hadn't come riding by."

"Gone for help," he said matter-of-factly.

"And might not have made it back in time to save General."

"I disagree. You're a resourceful woman, Reese."

"How would you know? We're not exactly friends."

Except he'd witnessed one of the worst moments in her life and had treated her secret like it was his own, telling no one. Did that give them some sort of bond?

"It shows." He angled his head in a way managing to be both confident and boyishly charming.

"I'm not that capable."

"No? You're the trustee of my father's estate. If you ask me, that's pretty resourceful."

Ah. There they were. The knives. And here she'd assumed they might have a normal conversation. "Believe it or not, I had nothing to do with your father's decision."

"Other than you returned to Mustang Valley and took a job at the bank a few weeks before he revised his will."

She stiffened. "A coincidence."

"Right."

"I can count on one hand the number of times I spoke to your father. The last was when he came into the bank and met with Walt, the manager. For the record, I wasn't in the meeting."

"Yet you were named as trustee."

"The bank was. I'm performing the duties because I'm assistant manager." Not entirely true, but Reese wasn't ready to reveal any private agreements between August and the bank.

"Does your father know?"

Reese stood straighter. "He doesn't."

"But he will soon enough."

"Gabe, I didn't strike up a conversation with you to bicker."

"Then why?"

There it was again, that flash of heat in his eyes. Darn him and darn her susceptibility.

"How well do you know your brothers?"

Her question elicited a sharp laugh.

"Have you had a chance to talk with them these last few days?"

"I've had the chance. Not the inclination." He studied her intently.

Reese resisted his close scrutiny. "I sense an animosity from them."

"No kidding." Gabe's tone rang with sarcasm.

"I'm serious. Josh and Cole appear to be… unhappy with the terms of the will."

"They aren't alone."

"I think Cole is only after money."

"What are you after?"

This wasn't going how Reese had hoped. She considered a different approach when Gabe's glance suddenly cut to the left.

"Quiet," he murmured and visibly tensed.

Reese peered over her shoulder. Josh and Cole weren't three feet away. Both wore suspicious expressions. How much, if anything, had they heard?

Gathering her wits, she said, "There you are. I was telling Gabe, the four of us need to schedule a meeting to review the financial records and discuss your father's plan for the ranch."

"We were about to suggest the same thing."

Josh looked to his brother. "We have some questions."

"What kind of questions?" Gabe demanded, his jaw tightening.

Placing herself between the three men, Reese plastered a smile on her face. "How's tomorrow afternoon at the ranch? Say, two o'clock?"

Chapter 3

Gabe watched Reese bid goodbye to his mother and Hector, fetch her coat and purse from the back of a dining room chair and leave by the front door.

A moment later, when no one was looking, he followed her, catching up as she reached her parked car in the driveway.

"Reese."

She stopped and turned, her car key clutched in her fingers. "Oh, did I forget something?"

"You by chance have a second?"

"Sure."

She looked anything but sure. A second later, she popped the locks on her Honda sedan. Opening the car door, she deposited her purse on the passenger seat, then waited.

"Why didn't you tell me yesterday you were the trustee?" he asked.

She crossed her arms over her middle. "My instructions were not to tell anyone before the reading of the will."

"I helped you rescue your horse."

"Doesn't work that way, Gabe."

He shifted, the chilly November air penetrating his dress shirt. Why hadn't he grabbed his suit jacket before coming outside?

"Isn't there a conflict of interest?"

"Rest assured, I'm completely unbiased when it comes to my job, and completely professional."

"Your father has been after Dos Estrellas for years. Twice he tried to buy it when Dad fell behind on the property taxes. And he made an offer earlier this year. Dad was going through chemo. Nothing like kicking a man when he's down."

"What are you implying?"

"Can you be relied on not to use your position to advance your father's ambitions?"

She pivoted on her high heels. It was a miracle she didn't lose her balance and face-plant in the driveway. "I'm going to pretend you didn't say that."

Gabe took hold of her elbow. They both stilled. "It's a fair question."

"I have never used my job to advance my father's ambitions or my own. Nor would I. You asking such a thing is insulting."

"Look at me, Reese." He waited until did. "I'm protecting my family."

She sagged, some of the fight going out of her. "You're angry—about the terms of the will and your brothers inheriting two-thirds of the ranch. You were also taken aback learning I'm the trustee. For those reasons, I'll pretend you didn't just question my ethics."

"Our fathers didn't get along."

"I disagree. They actually liked and admired each other greatly. My father has always spoken very highly of yours."

"They were business rivals. And your father was considerably more successful than mine."

"Your father had two families to support. I'm an only child, and my mother left when I was eight. It makes a difference."

Her parents' divorce was another similarity they shared. While Gabe's father had taken a mistress, Reese's mother had abandoned her family, running away with her lover, who was, at the time, the Small Change's tax accountant.

"And your father came from money," Gabe said.

"Which gave him all the more reason to admire yours. August Dempsey made something of himself from humble beginnings."

Gabe didn't voice what was on his mind, that, in the end, his father had lost much of what he'd built. The family would be paying off his medical bills for years. Which meant Reese would be the trustee of his father's estate for a long, long time.

"Can we not argue about this?" She glanced down at her arm, which Gabe still held.

He let his hand drop and instantly missed the intimate contact. He'd felt warmth beneath the fabric of her jacket. And soft, supple flesh. It had stirred his senses.

"Does your boss know about the feud between our families?"

"Of course he does."

"And he doesn't care?"

"First of all, I'm the one who told Walt. I thought it would be best he hear it from me. Secondly, as I said earlier, I'm required by my position with the bank to be honest and fair.

Also, every detail of my work will be scrutinized by the board." She squared her shoulders. "Should even one small detail come under question, my job could be at stake. I won't risk it."

"You don't need to work. Your father's well-off."

Reese inhaled sharply. "You're hardly an expert on my personal life."

Gabe could have kicked himself. "I'm sorry. I was out of line."

"Fine. Apology accepted." She reached for the open car door. "Now, if you don't mind."

"Would I also be out of line if I requested someone else at the bank be appointed as trustee? Surely, you aren't the only person qualified."

He expected her to be mad. She fooled him again by dismissing his question with an indifferent shrug. "You can ask. The answer will be no."

"Why?"

"I'm not at liberty to say."

"Sounds like a convenient excuse."

"It isn't."

Again, she'd barely reacted. Gabe found that interesting. Reese was either incredibly confident or she knew something she wasn't telling.

Her cell phone chimed from her jacket pocket. Extracting the phone, she glanced at the display and promptly answered with an anxious, "Yes, Enrico." After a pause, she said, "I'll be right there," and disconnected. "I have to go," she told Gabe.

"Is everything okay?"

"Yes. No." She fumbled with the phone before returning it to her pocket. "My father fell from the porch steps."

"Is he hurt?"

"Banged his knee. He may need to see the doctor."

For a banged knee? Gabe thought Reese might be overreacting. Theo McGraw was tough as nails and wouldn't be bothered by a little tumble off the porch steps. "Call me if you need anything."

She narrowed her gaze. "Really? After raking me over the coals, you're offering to be the good neighbor?"

"I, um…"

He'd started to say he was concerned for her, then changed his mind at the last second. He didn't give a damn about Reese McGraw.

Except, that wasn't true. He did feel something for her. Compassion and sympathy, at least. Why else would he have kept her secret all these years?

If not for their fathers' rivalry, their relationship might have taken a different path. They had been classmates and neighbors. Dating in high school wouldn't have been far-fetched.

Anything transpiring between them now, however, was out of the question, and Gabe was wise to maintain a safe distance.

The problem was he wanted to take her in his arms, give her a hug and tell her not to worry. Her father was going to be fine.

"I don't hate you, Reese. And I don't wish your father ill. If he needs help, or you, call me."

"Thank you." She slid onto the driver's seat, her hands gripping the steering wheel. "I'll see you tomorrow at two."

Aware he was crossing an invisible line, Gabe covered one of her white-knuckled hands with his. She was obviously worried about her father. "Drive careful. It's getting dark."

For a moment, they remained where they were. If Gabe didn't know better, he'd think a part of her wanted to stay. But that was ridiculous.

Whatever spell they'd fallen under ended, and she started the engine. Gabe watched her depart, thinking he should return to the house. Why, then, didn't he? At the end of the long road leading from the ranch house to the main road, Reese's brake lights illuminated. She turned left, in the direction of the Small Change.

He might have spent more time contemplating why her father's seemingly minor fall prompted her to leave in such a hurry except he was interrupted by the last person he wanted to see. His brother Josh.

Dammit. What did the man want now? The shirt off Gabe's back?

"Hope I didn't interrupt anything."

Gabe ground his teeth together. His brother's timing was impeccable. Or, perhaps, intentional. He could have spotted Gabe and Reese from the living room window.

"You didn't." Gabe pushed past him. Whatever Josh wanted, he wasn't interested.

"Got a minute?"

Gabe halted and cursed under his breath. "For what?"

They'd hardly spoken these past few days

despite living in close quarters. Gabe had no intention of changing the status quo.

"You and her," Josh hitched his chin in the direction Reese had driven in her car, "are you friends?"

Gabe's hackles rose. His relationship with Reese was no one's business. Especially Josh's.

"We're neighbors."

"I know. I lived here once."

He couldn't help thinking the reference to Josh residing at the ranch before Gabe came to live there was intentional.

"What I'm asking is, are you close?"

He stared his brother down.

Josh held his own. "It's a reasonable question. She's going to control the ranch's finances. If you and Reese are involved, there could be a conflict of interest."

Five minutes ago, Gabe had been asking Reese the same question. Now he defended her.

"She's a professional. She won't do anything to jeopardize her position at the bank."

"But you're friends."

"I'm not discussing her with you." Gabe once again started for the house and once again, Josh halted him with his words.

"I don't like this any better than you."

"We have nothing in common."

"Other than our father and this ranch and the fact we have to work together. Or agree to sell."

That rankled Gabe. "I'm not selling."

"Think about it before you decide. Dad left us with a lot of bills to pay and little means at our disposal. Selling would get us out of debt and free us to move on."

"There's no *we* as far as I'm concerned. Our father promised me the ranch. Not you and your brother."

Josh inhaled deeply as if to control his temper. "Cole and I have every right to inherit a share of Dos Estrellas."

"Because why? We happen to share the same blood?" Gabe snorted in disgust. "You haven't set foot on this place for twenty-four years."

"He cheated on my mother."

Josh had targeted Gabe's one weak spot, and the blow inflicted the desired damage.

He knew with all his heart his father had loved his mother deeply. That didn't make it right for him to disregard his marriage vows. Gabe's mother had raised him to be honorable. It was hard for him to accept the fact his father hadn't divorced his wife before becoming involved with Gabe's mother.

He'd asked once when he was twelve. His mother's face had immediately hardened, and she told him to never, ever bring up the subject again or she'd tan his hide. It was a private matter between her and his father.

In his early twenties, Gabe approached his father and got no further with him. The reason his father gave for not marrying his mother—that Gabe's maternal grandfather was very traditional and didn't approve— smacked of an excuse. When Gabe pressed, his father had stormed from the room. Only the love and devotion he felt for both his parents kept him from resenting them.

"We're done talking." Gabe strode ahead without looking back.

Good manners dictated he should return to the house and tell Hector goodbye. The attorney had been his father's closest confidant. But, like yesterday, Gabe needed an outlet to vent his frustration.

It was too late and too dark for a ride in the nearby mountains. Not too late to clean out the tack room, he decided. Nothing beat tossing a few crates and harnesses around to burn off steam. Dress shirt be damned.

"I remember," Josh called after him. "It was you who punched me in the nose at school. You had a pretty good right hook for a kid."

Gabe didn't miss a step, though it was the first thing his brother had said that made him smile.

Reese opened the jewelry box on her bedroom dresser, lifted out the top tray and removed a tiny framed picture hidden beneath. It was a ritual. Every year on this day, Celia's birthday, Reese studied the picture of her newborn daughter, let the memories of her birth warm her heart and then placed a phone call.

Today, Reese came home from the bank during her lunch hour in order to call Celia, but also to check on her father. His tumble off the porch yesterday could have been worse. Luckily, he hadn't fallen far, but he had *landed* hard and badly bruised his knee. Loss of balance was a common side effect of Parkinson's. As was stooped posture. Her father looked ten years older than he had mere months ago. She'd also noticed a slight tremor in his right hand and a quiver in his voice. Each new symptom increased her despair.

Feeling the weight of the little silver frame

in her hand, Reese stared at Celia's infant face and was reminded of why she'd excused herself after lunching with her father and retreated to her bedroom. How could she not be thinking of her daughter on this special day? The problem with Parkinson's was it consumed the thoughts of the person afflicted with it, along with their family members.

While Celia's parents made no secret of her adoption, they and Celia were the only ones who knew Reese was her birth mother. Shortly after her high school graduation, Reese had moved to Oregon to live with her older cousin Megan on the pretense of taking a year off before college. There, she'd given birth to Celia, who was then adopted by Megan and her husband.

They adored Celia. They also encouraged her to have a relationship with Reese, for which Reese felt grateful and blessed.

Ever since Celia could talk, Reese called her on a prearranged day once a month. Three times over the years, she'd flown to Oregon for a visit. In her closet, Reese kept a small trunk filled with letters from Celia, drawings, cards, photographs and, lately, school papers. Her computer contained numerous picture files organized by age.

Someday, when they were both ready, Celia would come to Mustang Valley for a visit and to meet her grandfather. Reese hoped it was soon, before the Parkinson's advanced to the point her father couldn't function or communicate.

"Hi, sweet pea," Reese said when Celia answered the phone. "Happy eleventh birthday."

"Reese! You called."

"Of course." Reese bit back a sob. Her emotions were getting the best of her today. "It sounds like you have a cold."

"We were supposed to go out for pizza tonight." Celia snuffled. "Now we have to wait for the weekend."

"That's too bad."

"I got your present. Thank you. The boots are exactly the ones I wanted."

They talked for twenty minutes until Reese had to say goodbye. The meeting at Dos Estrellas was scheduled for two, and she wanted to check on her father one last time before leaving.

"I hope you feel better soon," she said.

"Me, too. But I get to miss school, so that part's good."

Reese enjoyed their easy banter. "Send me pictures of the pizza party."

"I will. Goodbye, Reese."

"Goodbye, sweet pea." Reese disconnected before softly saying, "I love you." She and Celia weren't quite close enough for her to speak the words. Not yet, anyway. Maybe one day. She refused to push.

In the kitchen, she found her father sitting at the table, having his customary afternoon coffee.

"I thought the doctor said caffeine was bad for you," she scolded.

"Would you rather I have a whiskey?"

"Dad!"

"I've given up everything worthwhile. You're not taking away my coffee."

"Fine." She patted his shoulder and kissed the top of his head. "I won't tattle on you."

"Your Aunt Louise sent me an email earlier. She wants to come for a visit at Christmas."

"Great!" Reese's mood brightened. She adored her father's younger sister, who'd been like a second mother to her after her parents divorced. "How long's she going to stay?"

"I told her no. That we were busy."

"What!" Reese dropped into the chair across from her father and gaped at him.

"It's not a good time."

"You can't hide your Parkinson's forever."

"I'm not ready to tell her."

"It won't be Christmas without family visiting."

"Your Aunt Louise is a busybody. Always thinks she knows what's best for people."

"She loves you."

"She'll interfere."

Reese bit her tongue. Her father was the one sick, not her. It was his choice whom he told and when, regardless if she disagreed.

"Off to your meeting at Dos Estrellas?" He was attempting to distract her, and she let him.

"Depending on how long the meeting lasts, I may come straight home and skip going back to the bank."

"I'm still trying to wrap my brain around you being the trustee of August Dempsey's estate."

She'd finally informed her father last night, when she was able to do so. "Strange, I know."

"August must be having himself one heck of a good laugh up in heaven."

"He did choose the bank to act as trustee."

"Probably didn't realize you'd be the one running the show."

There was no way for Reese to respond

without violating her client's privacy, so she said nothing.

"Poor man," her father said. "He must have hated seeing the ranch fall to ruin like it did."

"Dos Estrellas is hardly in ruins."

"It's buried in debt."

Buried was an exaggeration. Waist-deep, maybe. "I can't discuss the ranch finances with you."

"He should have sold it to me when he had the chance."

Reese shook her head. "And what would you do with Dos Estrellas? Let's be honest, you're having enough trouble running the Small Change."

He grunted in displeasure. "Don't count me out yet."

"Never." She smiled and kissed his head again before retrieving her briefcase and a travel mug of coffee from the counter. "I'll see you later."

"Good luck," he called after her.

Reese passed Enrico on the way to her car, and they exchanged hellos. The ranch foreman was heading inside to give her father a report. The loyal employee had been doing that more and more of late, three or four times a day. And because her father was being regularly checked on, Reese was able to leave the house, confident he'd be all right.

In the indeterminable future, whether her father agreed or not, they would need to hire a caretaker. Reese could anticipate how their conversation would go and was dreading it.

During the ten-minute drive to Dos Estrellas, she mentally prepared for the meeting. This, she realized, was the third day in a row she'd see Gabe. She should get used to it. With her new responsibilities, they would be in frequent contact. The notion gave her a not-so-small shiver of anticipation—which she promptly squashed. Her attraction to Gabe was inappropriate, and even if they were to date, the timing couldn't be worse. He had a ranch in serious financial trouble to run alongside two brothers he didn't get along with.

Reese slowed to take the turn into the Dos Estrellas driveway. She parked in the same spot as yesterday, instantly reminded of her and Gabe's awkward, yet strangely intimate, parting. She'd have sworn he was about to say something revealing and romantic to her. When he didn't, she blamed her overactive imagination playing tricks on her.

But there was that moment between them

on the hilltop when he'd fastened her into the poncho...

Enough, she told herself. *This has to stop.*

Raquel Salazar answered Reese's knock on the door, smiling affectionately. "Come in, *chiquita.*"

Little girl? Reese could hardly call herself that. Raquel, however, was the motherly type who called everyone by an endearment.

"I have the office all set for you." Raquel indicated a door off the living room. "This way."

August's home office was a masculine mixture of functional and comfortable. Situated behind a heavy antique desk was an oversized executive chair. It nearly swallowed Reese when she sat down. Certificates lined one wall. August, it appeared, had been a member of several professional organizations, including the Arizona Cattlemen's Association.

On the other wall hung family portraits spanning several decades, back to the first Dempsey who'd originally purchased the land and built the ranch. A well-worn leather couch sat beneath the portraits and looked cozy enough to sink into for long hours of reading or listening to the old-fashioned stereo system.

Notably absent was evidence of modern technology. No computer. No TV, flat-screen or otherwise. No smartphone docking station or Bluetooth speaker. In fact, the one phone was an antiquated desktop model with a push-button dial pad, and the clock required a weekly winding to run.

Reese glanced around the room. "Where did August keep the ranch records?"

"In here." Raquel walked to a black lateral filing cabinet adjacent to the couch and opened the top drawer.

Reese could see rows and rows of hanging file folders with various headings: Payroll, Vehicles, Insurance, Veterinary Care, to name a few. "What about the financial information?"

"Ah." Raquel pulled out an elongated brown binder, which she placed on the desk in front of Reese. "Do you mean this?"

"Wow." Reese opened the binder and stared in amazement at the three-to-a-page checks and the thick stack of stubs. "I didn't know anybody used manual checks anymore."

"August didn't trust computers."

"So I see." Reese sighed, flipping through

the stubs and noting the entries. "What about income? How did he track that?"

Raquel opened a side drawer of the desk. Inside were a half dozen green accounting ledger books stacked one on top of the other.

"Great." Reese definitely had her work cut out for her. "Prior year tax returns handy?"

Those were in the next drawer down. Reese was relieved to see they'd been prepared by a local CPA.

Thankfully, Hector Fuentes had given her a flash drive with August's plan for the ranch, including a month-by-month and year-by-year schedule. Reese wasn't sure what she'd have done with handwritten notes.

"I'll tell the boys you're here," Raquel said and left, her footsteps soundless on the thick, colorful area rug.

Reese removed her laptop from her briefcase and powered it up. She also pulled out a copy of the entire living trust. When, a few minutes later, no one had yet arrived, she began examining the first accounting journal. It was meticulously updated until four months ago. After that, the entries were sketchy, then they stopped altogether.

August had probably gotten too sick to continue, which didn't bode well for the ranch finances.

Cole entered the office, removing his cowboy hat and running a hand through his windblown blond hair. Not the person Reese expected to see first.

"Hi." She greeted him in her best assistant bank manager smile. "Have a seat."

Raquel had brought in three chairs from the dining room and placed them across from the desk. Cole chose the one on the right and, sitting, balanced his hat on his knee.

"Will this take long?" he asked.

"I'm not sure. Depends on a number of things."

"Like?" He couldn't have a bigger chip on his shoulder if he tried.

"The number of questions you all have. How quickly we get through reviewing the records. What shape they're in." Terrible, these past four months. "How cooperative you are."

He answered by slouching in the chair, crossing his boots at the ankles and his arms over his stomach.

Reese wasn't impressed or intimidated.

Gabe entered the office next with Josh right behind him. If she didn't know better, she'd think they arrived together. But that was impossible, right?

"Hey, Reese." Josh grinned affably before taking the middle chair. "It is okay if I call you Reese?"

"Of course," she replied, trying not to stare at Gabe like a love-struck teenager.

He'd clearly come from the pastures or barn or wherever it was he'd been working. He smelled of the outdoors and looked ruggedly handsome with his tanned complexion and two-day growth of beard. With a nonchalance both unconscious and incredibly sexy, he sat, rolled down his shirtsleeves and rebuttoned them at the cuffs, but not before Reese caught sight of strong, prominently muscled arms with a light dusting of hair.

She remembered those arms from when they'd held her the night of their senior prom. She'd thought then they were the kind of arms a woman could rely on to take care of her and keep her safe.

"Are we ready to start?" Thankfully, her voice didn't betray the riot of emotions warring inside her.

Chapter 4

Gabe listened as Reese read from a document on her laptop computer. His father's plan for Dos Estrellas. Given the amount of detail, he'd trusted his legitimate sons no more than he'd trusted Gabe acting alone to make the right decisions for the ranch.

If it were possible for Gabe to move farther away from Josh without being obvious, he would. Why his mother had felt the need to place the chairs within inches of each other, he didn't know. To promote comradery was his guess. As if sitting close would dissolve years of animosity and resentment.

Admittedly, Gabe's opinion of Josh had

risen the smallest fraction yesterday following his remark about Gabe's right hook. Cole, well, he continued to annoy Gabe. The guy took attitude to a new level with a temper to match. To be fair, he probably thought the same thing about Gabe. And, no, that didn't make them brothers or even pals. Simply two people with good reason to be angry at each other.

Struggling to stay focused, he concentrated on Reese. It didn't help. She was far too distracting.

Today, she wore dress slacks and a tan sweater that, despite being bulky, hinted at the lovely, lush figure beneath. She wore minimal makeup—something Gabe preferred. Her one exception, pink lipstick accentuating a very kissable mouth.

Come to think of it, the other day on the mountain she hadn't been wearing any lipstick, and Gabe had still thought her mouth was kissable. Was every red-blooded male who came into the bank like him, appreciating her looks?

He supposed his brothers were entertaining similar thoughts. Josh had intimated as much yesterday, and Cole was practically licking his chops, which didn't sit well with Gabe. Was she noticing Cole in return?

Gabe's sudden sense of possessiveness regarding Reese made him pause. He had no claims *on* her and no interest *in* her, other than as the trustee of the Dempsey Living Trust. Best he remember that.

"Your father's first recommendation," Reese said, "is to sell off any excess cattle."

"Which we've already done." Gabe's remark had everyone turning in his direction. "This past fall we sold off about a quarter of the herd. Had to in order to pay for Dad's treatment."

At his mother's insistence, they'd admitted his father to a cancer center in Tucson. There, he'd been poked and prodded and subjected to an array of experimental drugs. The treatment may have extended his father's life by a few weeks. It certainly hadn't improved the quality of it.

"Can we sell more cattle?" Cole asked.

"We're down to sixteen hundred head. If we deplete the herd any more, we won't have enough breeding stock for next year."

"Can we buy more cows when the time comes?"

The question came from Josh, and Gabe resisted a biting reply. His brother clearly hadn't been listening to any of their conversations this week.

"Not unless you have a way of printing money."

Reese rested her elbows on the desk. "Your father did establish a line of credit with the bank before he died, secured by the ranch. One hundred thousand dollars."

Gabe hid his surprise. He had no idea.

"But I would advise drawing on the line very conservatively until the ranch is generating enough income to cover the interest payments."

"Beef is high now anyway," Gabe said. The elevated prices had been good when it came to selling their stock, but would be bad for buying. "We'd be smarter to wait on buying more cows until the spring or next summer when prices drop."

"In that case," Reese continued, "we'll move to the next item on your father's list. Maintain the current herd through winter."

Gabe reined in his impatience. "Which is going to be a problem."

"How so?" Josh asked.

At his brothers' blank stares, Gabe said, "We've had no rain since last fall, and grass doesn't grow without water. At this rate, we'll have to buy hay and grain to supplement the grass or the herd will suffer."

Reese nodded thoughtfully. "I see."

Gabe wondered if she did see. She was the daughter of a cattle rancher and must have some idea about weather and its effect on grazing lands. The Small Change was in the same position as Dos Estrellas; they would need to buy supplemental feed, as well. There was one big difference. The Small Change wouldn't be buying supplemental feed with the last cent to their name.

"How much money is in the ranch checking account?" Cole asked.

The question irked Gabe, though he'd wondered the same thing. From what he'd seen of Cole, all his brother cared about was money and getting his hands on some. Reese had tried to warn him yesterday after the reading of the will, specifically, about Cole's wanting money rather than part ownership of the ranch.

Reese returned to her computer screen. After a minute, she said, "Less than ten thousand dollars, I'm afraid."

"What about his life insurance? Was there a policy?"

Gabe bristled. Cole didn't even have the decency to refer to their father as Dad.

"Yes." Reese returned Cole's probing stare. Kudos to her, thought Gabe. She had no fear. Then again, he'd seen her trying to pull a thousand-pound horse out of a sinkhole by herself. That was the definition of no fear. "The proceeds went to Raquel."

"Aren't they part of the estate?"

She shook her head. "Gabe's mother is the owner of the policy and the beneficiary."

"Is that legal?"

"Perfectly."

Cole's mouth turned down. He wasn't happy about the policy or Reese's clipped tone, but he said nothing.

Good thing. Gabe's mother had stood faithfully by his father for years, including the last two, which had been the hardest. She deserved something, and Gabe's father had wanted her to have a small nest egg. If Cole had objected, Gabe would have been compelled to give him more than a piece of his mind.

Last night, over coffee, his mother had hinted at giving the money to Gabe. He'd refused and not because of his father's wishes. With all their futures uncertain, he, too, wanted his mother to have some money to fall back on.

"The next item on your father's plan is to slowly increase the herd."

"How do we accomplish that if we've sold off a quarter of the cattle and can't buy more?" Unlike his younger brother, there was no rancor in Josh's voice.

"Aggressive breeding," Gabe answered for Reese. "And choosing the right time of year."

"What determines that?"

"Availability of feed and beef prices."

"Which are high." Josh said.

He appeared interested, but Gabe remained skeptical. It would take a lot more than a token show of interest to change his mind about either of his brothers.

"Prices are high today," he said. "But they can change in a matter of weeks. And, like I mentioned before, weather's affected the growth of grass. Poor feed results in poor-quality cattle. Whatever extra money we have will pay for grain and hay. There's also the matter of land. Each acre can feasibly sustain only so many cattle. Right now, with a shortage of grass, it's about two head."

"That's all?"

Josh's question showed just how little he

and Cole knew about the cattle industry. What was their father thinking when he left them two-thirds of the ranch? Gabe had his work cut out for him. He could either try to teach them the cattle business or watch them fail and drag him down, too.

There was a third choice. They could sell Dos Estrellas. And a potential buyer, Theo McGraw, was the father of the estate's trustee.

No. The latter two choices weren't options. Gabe refused to lose the ranch. Not to his brothers' glaring inadequacies and especially not to his father's archrival.

"What about the mustang sanctuary?" Josh asked. "With more land, we may not need to purchase supplemental feed."

Gabe scrubbed his face and groaned. Was the man not listening yesterday during the reading of the will?

"That land belongs to Cara."

"Technically," Josh said slowly, "it belongs to us."

"It's hers to use indefinitely." As long as they didn't sell the ranch.

Josh addressed Reese. "You're the trustee. You have control over the ranch's assets. If the land was returned to the ranch, we could buy more cattle and expand the herd."

"The bank's position is, barring extenuating circumstances, to follow the terms of the will to the letter." Reese closed her laptop. "I think demanding Cara give up the sanctuary is premature. You have the line of credit and several months to make a go of this."

Cole sat up straighter. "Maybe we should sell the ranch."

"No!" Gabe all but shouted his refusal.

"Fine. Then buy us out. We're allowed to sell our shares."

Gabe had read the will. He knew the terms. And what he'd give for the kind of money required to buy out his brothers. "Believe me, I would if I could."

"I'll cut you a deal."

Gabe knew what he wanted more than anything. "Give me six months, and I'll have the money."

"I'd rather sell now."

Before he could answer, Josh cut in. "I'm not ready to sell yet, either."

Wow. Really? That was hardly the response Gabe expected.

"Since when?" Cole demanded. "You need the money more than me."

Josh worked his jaw as if contemplating his brother's remark, then said to Reese, "I have two children. A boy, two and a half, and a girl, nine months. I'm in the process of gaining full custody. To satisfy the court, I need a permanent place to call home. Dos Estrellas fits the bill."

She smiled pleasantly. Almost wistfully. "There's nowhere better than Mustang Valley to raise a family."

Was she encouraging him to stay? Gabe suffered a stab of betrayal, though he had no reason. He and Reese weren't intimate or even friends. They were barely acquaintances.

"I need to go home for a few days," Josh said. "Maybe a week. Get more of my things. I'll be back before Thanksgiving."

"What about Brawley?" Cole asked.

Gabe wasn't a rodeo enthusiast, but he knew from overhearing Josh and Cole this morning at breakfast that Brawley, California, was home of the Cattle Call Rodeo.

"Looks like I'm making a career change. Ranching for rodeoing."

"Good luck," Cole grumbled.

"You, too, little brother. You're coming back here with me."

Josh's declaration wasn't well received, judging by Cole's scowl. By Gabe, either.

Given his choice, both brothers would return to California and stay. Indefinitely.

Since they weren't likely to leave, the next best thing would be for him to acquire full ownership. For that, he'd have to come up with a game plan, and fast. Thanksgiving, and his brothers' return, was right around the corner.

"Get along little dogies, get along."

Hearing Violet's singing, Gabe laughed to himself. Dos Estrellas's livestock manager couldn't carry a tune to save her life. Then there was her song choice.

Pushing the four stragglers through the gate and into the next section of grazing land wasn't exactly the same as driving a herd of cattle across open range. But he appreciated her enthusiasm.

"We're done here," he called to Violet once the last young heifer meandered through the gate, lowing softly to her mates ahead.

"Okay, boss." Violet dismounted. Whistling the same tune she'd been singing, and just as off-key, she closed the wide gate and shoved the latch into place.

Boss. Gabe liked the sound of that. Ranch employees had called his father boss. What would they call his brothers, if anything? More interesting, what did they think of the brothers' part ownership and their staying on to run the place with Gabe?

It had been three days since Josh and Cole had left for California. Josh had called yesterday to say they'd be returning Thanksgiving Eve. Gabe was admittedly enjoying the peace and quiet. For now, and for the next few days, at least, he was the sole boss of Dos Estrellas.

Violet mounted and rode up beside him. Gabe nudged Bonita into a brisk walk. After some debate, he and Violet had decided to move the herd to a different section of grazing land, allowing the depleted vegetation in this section to regrow. With the help of their three best hands, the operation had gone smoothly, taking them all of yesterday and half of this morning.

The exception was a couple dozen strays who'd decided they'd rather hide in a stand of trees near the stock pond. These last four cattle were the most stubborn of the lot. And the craftiest. In the end, Gabe and Violet had prevailed.

"I have some news for you," she said, her jaw working as she chewed on a piece of dried grass.

"What's that?"

"It's about Mickey."

Violet had worked at Dos Estrellas for the past ten years, since she was eighteen. Gabe's father had originally hired her on as a wrangler. She'd worked her way up, from head wrangler to assistant livestock manager to senior livestock manager right before Gabe's father had become sick.

And while every bit a cowboy on the outside, she was one hundred percent girl on the inside. Back when she'd first started at the ranch, Gabe had asked her out. They'd gone on a few dates before mutually deciding they made better friends than romantic partners.

Gabe's father had also liked Violet, which was one reason he'd continually promoted her. The other was that she outperformed every other wrangler on the place, rightfully earning each of her new positions.

"What's with Mickey now?" Gabe didn't have a lot of patience when it came to the young wrangler, who worked hard one day and loafed off the next.

"He's leaving at the end of the week." Violet tossed away the stalk of dried grass. "Told me this morning."

"Not much notice."

"Said he got a better offer."

Gabe had his doubts. "From who?"

"Miracle Mile. They're near Tonopah."

He'd heard of the ranch. A little bigger than Dos Estrellas, but with a less-than-stellar reputation.

"Good luck to him."

Violet raised her brow, her head bobbing in rhythm to the horse's easy gait. "You're not mad?"

"Naw. Mickey's better off at Miracle Mile, and we're better off without him."

"Leroy's talking about leaving, too."

That did concern Gabe. "Why?"

"If you don't mind me saying, boss, the guys are a little worried. Talk is, money's in short supply, and what's left is going to the California Dempseys."

California Dempseys? That was what the employees called Gabe's brothers? Better than the California owners.

"I won't lie," Gabe said. "We aren't rolling in dough. But there's enough to carry the ranch for the next several months. I'm working on a longer-term solution."

"Good. I'll let the guys know."

"If they have a problem or want answers, they can come to me. I'll tell it to them straight."

"Wouldn't expect anything less from you."

Violet's respectful demeanor gave Gabe a warm feeling inside. It also motivated him to take action. His goal to buy his brothers' share wouldn't come together on its own.

Watching the last four strays reunite with the herd grazing contentedly on the green, rolling hills, Gabe envisioned what lay ahead and the course he must take. Cattle were what sustained the ranch, and increasing the herd was the best way to boost revenue.

"Can you finish up here?" he asked Violet. "I've got an appointment in town."

"Sure thing."

He trotted Bonita down the rocky rise and most of the way back to the barn. He hadn't been fibbing to Violet. He did have an appointment in town. Reese simply didn't know about it yet.

Smelling of cows was no way to make an impression. After unsaddling Bonita and returning her to the horse stable, he headed to the house. He showered and changed into clean jeans and a dress shirt.

Luckily, Cara was busy with some new arrivals at the mustang sanctuary and his mother had gone shopping in nearby Rio Verde for Thanksgiving dinner. Gabe could leave without having to answer their well-intended but nosy questions, about where he was going and why.

At the bank, he was informed by the teller that Reese was with a customer and he'd have to wait.

"How long will she be?"

"I'm not sure." The teller, a young man Gabe had seen on occasion, checked the wall clock. "Probably not long."

Gabe sat in one of the waiting chairs near an overly decorated seven-foot Christmas tree. Already? It wasn't even Thanksgiving yet. He'd noticed decorations in several store-fronts on his way in, plus an empty lot next to the market cordoned off in preparation of tree sales. Signs for the community-wide annual Holly Daze Festival starting in a couple of weeks were posted all over town.

He typically didn't bother with the festival, but his mother had been talking about going for weeks. She'd missed last year's because of his father's illness. Gabe supposed he'd be the one recruited to take her and Cara.

His seat in the bank waiting area did offer one advantage: an unobstructed view of Reese's office. Through the floor-to-ceiling glass panel, he saw her sitting behind her desk, engaged in conversation with the customer who wasn't visible behind the solid wood door.

Hmm. She didn't look happy. If Gabe were to venture a guess, this particular customer was pushing all her hot buttons.

Well, finances could be a touchy subject. If she were turning down a loan request or collecting on a delinquent account, the person might be giving her grief. Gabe sat back in the deep cushioned chair and continued watching, intrigued by her expressive face.

She was lovely. Quite beautiful, actually, and obviously smart. Poised and confident. How had she flown so far under his radar until now? It wasn't like he hadn't seen her periodically, from a distance anyway, since her return. Probably because they worked diligently at avoiding each other.

Gabe noticed Reese twirling a pen between her thumb and forefinger as if venting her anger. Was she bored by her customer? No, Gabe clearly saw her face from where he sat, and her eyes were snapping. Whoever this customer was, he or she was getting to Reese while she struggled to maintain her cool.

Yet another quality to like about her. They were starting to stack up. Oh, yeah. Except for that one little obstacle: her tight grip on the Dos Estrellas purse strings.

The next instant, the door to her office flew open, startling Gabe. He glanced up and stared openly. The person with Reese was no customer. Blake Nolan strode angrily out of the office, his features dark and menacing.

He and Gabe were casually acquainted. Blake's mother was one of the town supervisors, and Gabe's father, like many of the local ranchers, had dealt frequently with the board of supervisors. Today, however, Gabe and Blake might have been complete strangers, for the other man walked past him without saying a word.

Gabe rose, considered hailing Blake, then thought better of it. He was more interested in Reese, how she was doing and—okay, fine— what had transpired between her and Blake.

He started for her office.

"Sir," the teller called out. "If you'll give me a second to buzz Ms. McGraw—"

"We're friends." At the door, he paused to take in Reese. "You all right?"

A flicker of surprise was her only reaction, which she quickly contained. "Gabe. What are you doing here? You're not on my calendar."

"I took a chance you were free."

"What can I do for you?"

He walked into her office and shut the door behind him.

She regarded him with suspicion. "Is this about the ranch?"

"You didn't answer my question. Are you all right?"

"Why wouldn't I be?" She tugged on the cuffs of her sweater, straightening the sleeves.

"Blake didn't appear very happy when he left."

"I'm not discussing him with you."

"Was it business or personal?" Gabe lowered himself into the visitor chair Blake had recently vacated.

"I repeat," she said in a clipped tone, "what are you doing here?"

He leaned forward. "I was concerned about you, is all."

"Because we're friends?" Though her tone remained clipped, her demeanor softened a bit around the edges. "I heard you say that to the teller."

"We're not?"

"We're business associates first."

"Funny isn't it?" He chuckled mirthlessly. "How did that happen, by the way?"

"Gabe, what do you want? I have another appointment in twenty minutes."

He sat back, striving to appear relaxed. In truth, he was a bundle of nerves. He'd sat in on several meetings with his father, always watching and learning, but he'd never conducted one. They'd both assumed his father had many more years ahead of him to run Dos Estrellas.

"I did some checking around this morning," Gabe said. "Made a few phone calls. Talked to a cattle broker. We can easily sustain five hundred more head. A thousand, even."

He waited for her to take what he saw as the logical leap. She didn't, simply stared at him and waited.

"I'd like to draw on the line of credit," he finally said.

"To purchase cattle?"

Was she intentionally baiting him? "Yes."

"Do your brothers know?"

"They're not back from California yet. Does it matter?"

"Yes. Any loans, including advances, must be approved of by all three owners." She didn't talk to him as if he were stupid or accuse him of not reading the will, which he appreciated.

That didn't lessen Gabe's frustration. "Can't you authorize it as the trustee?"

"Possibly. But I won't."

"This is a good time to buy. Beef prices are predicted to go up even higher."

Reese rested her clasped hands on the desk. "The ranch can't *easily* sustain more head, and you need the line of credit for supplemental feed."

"It could rain tomorrow. They're forecasting a ten percent chance."

She inhaled slowly. "I think we should wait. Stay the course for a few months. You said yourself at our recent meeting that summer is a better time to buy, when beef prices typically go down."

Gabe could also be stubborn. "Dad's plan was to grow the herd. You said so yourself."

"Slowly grow the herd," she reiterated.

"A few hundred head isn't exactly leaps and bounds."

"I'm sorry, Gabe."

"That's it?" He squeezed the chair's upholstered armrests hard enough to feel the metal bar inside. "You're in charge, so you can veto any request."

"I'll be glad to talk about it with all three of you when your brothers return."

And here he'd been thinking how attractive she was and smart. Right. He'd left out the part about her being obstinate and inflexible.

He abruptly stood. "Who's the manager here?"

"Walt Marshall." She also stood. "Why?"

"I want to talk to him about a change in trustee."

"It's not up to you. Your father named the bank."

"Then someone else here can take over. This Walt guy, for one."

Reese shook her head. "No, he can't."

"Why the hell not?" Gabe was getting pretty sick and tired of her countering everything he said.

"There are conditions."

"Like?"

"Gabe." She exhaled slowly. "I didn't want to tell you this." Her tone warned him not to ask.

He did anyway. "Tell me what?"

She hesitated. "Your father didn't just name Southern Arizona Bank as the trustee. He specifically requested me to oversee the trust."

"You're joking!"

"I'm afraid I'm not."

"How long have you known?"

"Since he arranged for the bank to be trustee."

He stared in amazement. "And you didn't say anything?"

"I couldn't. And even if bank policy didn't prohibit me, it wasn't my place."

"I don't believe you."

"Feel free to speak to Walt." She leaned back in her chair. "He'll tell you the same thing."

It was difficult for Gabe to see the sympathy in Reese's eyes through the red haze surrounding him. How could this be happening? Bad enough he had to share ownership of Dos Estrellas with two brothers who disliked him as much as he did them. He couldn't make a single decision about the ranch without the approval of Reese, the daughter of his father's rival.

None of this made sense. What could his father have been thinking? To specifically request Reese...

Gabe didn't say goodbye. Not that he remembered, anyway.

He knocked into the chair on his way out,

muttering a curse under his breath. The next thing he knew, he was behind the wheel of his truck and driving across town to the attorney Hector Fuentes's office.

Maybe Gabe could contest the will. Or, there was a loophole giving him leverage over Reese. He had to find out, and Hector was the only one able to give him the answer.

Chapter 5

"Smells great, Mom."

"Gabriel, *mijo*. Did you put the extra leaf in the dining room table?"

"All done."

"And move the flowers to the living room?"

"Yep." Over a week had passed since the funeral and there were a dozen-plus floral and plant arrangements still alive and thriving. Gabe knew his mother didn't have the heart to throw them out.

"Good," she pronounced. "Now Cara can finish with the place settings."

Opening the oven door, Raquel checked the turkey and sides roasting inside. A blast of warmth filled the kitchen, along with an array of incredibly delicious aromas.

"You need any help?" he asked.

"I'm okay for now. Maybe in a little while." She shut the oven door, wiped her forehead with the back of her oven-mitted hand and sighed.

Along with the turkey, stuffing, sweet potatoes, cranberry relish and pumpkin pie, his mother had prepared a pot of beans, another pot of rice, two dozen beef enchiladas and a bowl of the hottest homemade salsa this side of Mustang Valley. In lieu of rolls or bread, warm flour tortillas would be served.

The Dempseys and Salazars had been a culturally blended family for as long as Gabe could remember. Being originally from Hermosillo, Mexico, the Salazars didn't celebrate Thanksgiving. It was different for August Dempsey. The holiday had a special meaning because it fell near the date his grandfather had purchased the land for Dos Estrellas. To please him, Gabe's mother prepared a big dinner, substituting favorite Mexican dishes for other, more common, American ones.

Gabe wondered what his brothers would think of the unusual menu. They'd returned from California late yesterday afternoon, driving two trucks and hauling two trailers. One was a rented moving van containing their personal belongings. The other, a horse trailer. They'd brought six of their personal mounts, four of which were Cole's championship calf-roping horses.

Without trying to be obvious, Gabe had looked the horses over last night as his brothers unloaded them. All appeared fit and stout with an alertness shining in their eyes. They weren't, however, ranch horses, and there was a big difference between roping calves in the rodeo ring and herding them across open range.

They might be trainable. Time would tell. He decided to see how badly his brothers floundered before stepping in and giving them pointers.

Not his choice. Unfortunately, Gabe's visit to Hector's office last week had been a complete waste of time. The attorney, not bothering to hide his impatience with Gabe, assured him there was nothing to be done about either Gabe's brothers or Reese's position as trustee.

The sting had diminished, these past few days. Actually, who was he kidding? Gabe had chosen to ignore his frustration and anger rather than obsess about it. Perhaps after the holidays, when he had a better handle on the situation, he could try again.

Try what, exactly? Bang his head against the proverbial wall?

"*Mijo*, can you stir the beans for me?"

Grabbing the large wooden spoon, he did as his mother requested. There was hardly any space on the stove top. As usual, she'd prepared enough food to feed a small village.

Cara breezed into the kitchen. "The table's set. What else do you need, Tia Raquel?"

Gabe was glad to see her smiling. The holidays were difficult for her since she'd lost her young son two years ago. Gabe supposed it would be the same for him and his mother from now on.

"Where are Josh and Cole?" he asked.

"The backyard, last I checked." Cara stood on tiptoes and glanced out the window over the sink. "Yeah, they're sitting in the lawn chairs."

It annoyed Gabe that his brothers weren't inside with the rest of the family, helping with dinner or, at the least, socializing. Then again, he and Cara hadn't done much to make them feel welcomed. Just his mother.

"Cara, why don't you tell them we'll be ready to eat in about a half hour?"

"I think they're fine for the time being." Cara caught Gabe's eye and sent him the same conspiratorial look they'd often shared through the years. She was on his side and letting him know it.

The front doorbell rang.

"Who could that be?" Cara started across the kitchen.

With so many people showing up in recent weeks, and Gabe's brothers still settling in, his mother had suggested they limit dinner to immediate family. Gabe had heartily agreed.

"Let Gabe answer the door." His mother caught Cara by the shirtsleeve, and presented her with a strainer. "You drain the beans. My arthritis is bothering my hands."

Gabe had exactly one second to contemplate the oddness of his mother's remark—she'd been using her hands all day cooking without complaint—when the doorbell rang again.

"I'll get rid of them," Gabe said, already on his way.

"Nonsense." His mother's voice trailed after him. "Invite her in."

He didn't register his mother's use of the word *her* until he threw open the door. Seeing their guest, he silently cursed himself for not paying better attention.

Reese held a pink dessert box and a bottle of wine. Gabe stared like an idiot, struck dumb by her unexpected appearance and the killer tight jeans she wore, made sexier by her knee-high boots and a super-short jacket hugging her narrow waist. Her hair was pinned to the back of her head in a tidy knot that made Gabe think about removing the pins and sifting his fingers through the thick, silky strands.

If she had dressed like this the other day at the bank, he might not have been so angry at her for turning down his request.

After a moment, she tilted her head at an appealing angle. "Can I come in?"

"What are you doing here?"

She held up the dessert box and wine bottle. "These are for your mother. She invited me. Also my dad, but he can't make it."

"You're kidding." Gabe didn't know whether to be angry at his mom or impressed by her audacity. And at Reese's audacity for accepting the invitation. "Why would she do that?"

"I didn't ask her, but, if I was to venture a guess, I'd say she's trying to smooth out any difficulties in my working relationship with your family."

"Okay, but why did you agree to come?"

"The same reason."

He studied her one moment longer before standing back and allowing her to enter. He was glad he did for she gave off a hint of the most intriguing fragrance as she breezed past him.

One look at her walking away from him in those jeans and he wanted to investigate further.

She paused in the middle of the living room, waiting for him to catch up. He forced himself to not run.

"I'm sorry about the other day," she said. "I know you don't believe me, but I really didn't want to turn down your request."

"Too late now, the broker sold the cattle to another buyer."

"There'll be more cattle on the market. Maybe at a better price."

"And I'll still have to come begging to you with my hat in my hand."

"You didn't beg."

"And I never will." He hitched his chin toward the kitchen. "We're eating in the dining room, but everyone's in the kitchen."

Gabe was shocked his mother had invited Reese, and not because of the obvious reasons.

Their guests at holiday dinners were always close friends. Seldom family. The rift between Gabe's father and brothers wasn't the only one plaguing the Dempseys. His mother, while close to his grandmother, barely spoke to his grandfather. Gabe wasn't entirely sure of the reason for their estrangement, but he could guess. His *abuelo* Salazar hadn't approved of Gabe's father and the fact his mother began their relationship as an affair with a married man.

Gabe barely knew his maternal grandparents. They used to visit once a year in the summer when Gabe was little, staying at the bed-and-breakfast in town. That practice stopped years ago. They hadn't even attended August's funeral, though his grandmother had called, as she did frequently throughout the year.

"You first." Gabe gestured to Reese.

She walked confidently ahead of him into the kitchen. If she felt out of place or awkward, she didn't let it show. The same couldn't be said about his brothers. Since their return, their discomfort hung on them like ill-fitting shirts.

"You're here." Gabe's mother abandoned arranging the condiment tray and engulfed Reese in a friendly hug, which she returned as best she could with her hands full. "I'm so glad. How's your father?"

"He's sorry he couldn't come."

Gabe still couldn't believe his mother had invited Theo McGraw. Was she crazy? Maybe she was taking his father's death harder than he thought.

"These are for you." Reese held out the dessert box and wine to Raquel. "I hope you like pecan pie."

Gabe's mother beamed. "It was August's favorite."

How did Reese know that? Coincidence? Gabe wondered.

"Dad told me." She smiled warmly. "I guess August ordered it during the ranchers' monthly get-togethers at the Cowboy Up Café."

Gabe had attended those meetings numerous times with his father. August and Theo McGraw had always sat on opposite sides of the restaurant. Either Reese's father possessed superhuman vision and could see great distances or...

Was it possible the two men had been friendlier than they'd let on? His father had sometimes spoken well of Theo McGraw, when he wasn't cursing the other man's existence.

"Let me take that." His mother relieved Reese of the wine. "I'll put it in the refrigerator to chill. You can set the pie on the counter."

Gabe couldn't take his eyes off Reese. She busied herself with the pie, then flitted around the kitchen helping here and there as if she'd visited a hundred times before.

"Where's my china platter?" His mother had opened the cupboard and was staring at the top shelf.

"In the pine trunk, Tia Raquel." Cara, Gabe noticed, was also watching his mother, with the same bewilderment on her face he felt.

"Ah, yes." His mother closed the cabinet and smiled with satisfaction. "I forgot."

She normally had the memory of an elephant. But she'd had a lot on her mind lately. Gabe could understand her forgetting where she left something.

"Will you get it for me, Gabe? The trunk is in the garage."

"Sure."

"Take Reese with you. For an extra set of eyes."

The request smacked of a setup. That would explain how his mother seemingly forgot the location of the platter.

"I can manage, Mom."

"Nonsense. What else is Reese to do with herself?"

"I'd be happy to go with you," she said, giving Gabe reason to wonder if she was in on things.

No. His mother worked alone, never able to make an ally of him or Cara when it came to her often-outrageous schemes. Reese was probably innocent. Like him. But he wasn't ignorant. Whatever reason his mother had for getting him and Reese alone, he didn't care. Her plan would fail.

"All right," he said. "Follow me."

They walked from the kitchen, through the laundry room and out the door leading to the garage. Gabe flipped on the light switch and indicated a step down.

"Watch it." He resisted taking her hand.

The pine chest sat against the wall, covered

by an old quilt. In addition to the platter, his mother kept an assortment of other, seldom used, holiday relics.

Removing the quilt, Gabe lifted the lid on the chest, trying hard to ignore Reese's proximity. She didn't need to stand right beside him.

"I'm glad your mother suggested I go with you."

He straightened, one hand resting on the chest lid. "You are?"

"I was rude to you the other day at the bank. This gives us a chance to talk."

"We cleared the air when you first arrived."

"I wanted to tell you why Blake was at the bank."

Not what Gabe was expecting to hear. "Like you said, it's none of my business."

"Yes…and no. You're one of the few people besides him who knows I was pregnant."

"You don't have to tell me.

"You're right. But I'd like to. You've kept my secret a lot of years, and I appreciate it."

"Okay." Gabe closed the lid on the chest without removing the platter. He sat, then patted the spot next to him. "I'm listening."

What had seemed like a good idea now felt like a colossal mistake. Had she lost her mind, suggesting she and Gabe talk? Yes, she regretted having to decline his request for a draw on the line of credit. That was no reason to reveal her past and what occurred after the night of their senior prom.

She paced the garage floor in front of Gabe, not accepting his invitation to sit beside him. The pine chest was small. Okay, not minuscule. But if she sat beside him, they'd be elbow to elbow. Thigh to thigh. Hardly conducive to pouring her heart out.

"I promise not to bite," he said, tracking her every step.

Bite? Her throat felt suddenly dry as she imagined his teeth tugging playfully on her neck or on the inside of her arm. Swallowing didn't help.

"This is harder than I anticipated," she said.

Gabe grabbed her hand and tugged her onto the chest. Reese gasped softly. She'd been right. They were elbow to elbow. Thigh to thigh. His legs were strong and muscular, the result of hard physical labor every day of his life.

Her father had been strong once, with the build of a professional athlete. The Parkinson's had sucked every last ounce of strength out of him.

But that wasn't what she wanted to tell Gabe. Gathering her courage—they didn't have much time, dinner would be served soon—she began in a halting voice.

"The reason Blake stormed out of my office was because he didn't like my answer regarding his business with the bank."

"There's a lot of that going around."

She searched his face, unsure if he was teasing or serious. The corner of his mouth twitched ever so slightly. Teasing, she decided.

"It wasn't personal and wasn't about our daughter."

"Daughter?" Gabe studied her intently. "You had the baby, then?"

"Yes." She shifted, but there was no escaping. Short of her getting up, Gabe's body parts and hers would remain touching. With some effort, Reese refocused her attention. "And, to answer your next question, Blake knows about Celia."

Gabe shrugged. "I didn't ask."

"But you were wondering. His wife, Wynonna, knows, too."

"Did he tell her before or after they were married?"

"I never asked. It didn't matter."

"That must have been hard. Giving up your child. Or am I assuming wrong?"

She nodded. "You're right. About me giving her up and how hard it was. The hardest thing I've ever done." Even coping with her father's illness didn't compare. "But I was barely eighteen when she was born and incapable of providing for a child."

"Your father would have—"

"Not an option."

Reese would not discuss her family's complex dynamics with Gabe, and how disappointed and brokenhearted her straitlaced father would have been with her—for getting pregnant and having a relationship with an engaged man. She wouldn't have blamed him. But because of Celia, she didn't regret her actions. What she did regret was the difficult position she'd put Blake in, and she accepted full responsibility.

"Celia was adopted by my cousin Megan in Oregon," she continued. "We have a long-distance relationship. When the time's right, and Celia's ready, my cousin and I have agreed Celia can come to Mustang Valley for a visit. Hopefully, to meet my father."

"I thought he still didn't know about her."

"Things have…changed lately. I'm, well,

ready to tell Dad, and I think he'll be more receptive." She exhaled. "Celia's asked to meet him. Maybe after the first of the year. Or her spring break from school."

"What about Blake?"

"He's less inclined to establish a relationship with her."

Gabe called Blake an unflattering name under his breath.

"Don't be so quick to judge." Amazingly, once she got started, she found talking to Gabe not hard at all. "Blake was involved with Wynonna long before I pursued him. I knew he was engaged from the start." She took a moment to collect herself. "I was young and stupid and thought I was in love. To my shame, I took advantage of a rough patch he and Wynonna were going through. My mistake was in thinking he'd break off the engagement and not get back together with her. His mistake, too, I suppose, for leading me on."

"Whatever the circumstances, he's still Celia's father."

"And the father of two other children with his wife, who may not want to or be ready to accept Celia in their lives. I respect their choice."

"That's no excuse," Gabe insisted. "He has a responsibility."

"Not financially, he doesn't. Any obligation was eliminated when he consented to the adoption. That was part of our agreement."

"He has a kid living in Oregon and doesn't care enough to see her?"

Reese could see how Gabe related to Celia and superimposed his own feelings onto her. He was also the illegitimate child of a parent with two legitimate sons. The difference was Celia, who had no conflicting emotions.

"Actually, it's up to Celia. She and I talk regularly, and I've visited her a few times. She loves her mother and father, and isn't compelled to seek out her biological father."

"That could change."

Reese didn't disagree. "When and if it does, we'll figure things out. In the meantime, she's happy, which is the most a parent can hope for their child."

"Why are you telling me this, Reese?"

She sought the right words, needing Gabe to understand her reasons.

"I trust you."

"Huh. Didn't see that coming. I'm pretty sure I threatened you recently with having you removed as trustee."

"Oh, right."

He chuckled. "Am I to assume you aren't angry?"

"It was a knee-jerk reaction. Happens a lot at work." Returning his smile was difficult. Reese's nerves were getting to her. She and Gabe had never been like this before. Close physically and emotionally. "I trust you because you didn't tell anyone I was pregnant. That means something."

"What does it mean, Reese?"

The smooth timbre of his voice as he said her name caused a stirring in her middle. It was impossible to ignore and resist. Gabe was having an effect on her. And these intimate conversations they'd engaged in lately only heightened her awareness of, and attraction to, him.

He leaned in, and his breath caressed her cheek. She had to stop this. Right now. If not, they might be tempted to venture into dangerous territory.

"We should probably go inside." She made an effort to rise, but changed her mind when her shaky legs threatened to give out. "Your mom's expecting her platter."

"Not yet." He placed a hand on her arm.

"Gabe," she whispered right before his lips

found hers and covered them completely. Her eyes drifted shut as he increased the pressure of their kiss.

This could not be happening. But, it was, and Reese wasn't doing anything to stop Gabe or the incredible sensations his assault on her mouth elicited. Nor, would she stop him. Not yet, anyway. Another minute. Maybe two. The kiss was just too delicious. Too powerful. Too sensual. A soft moan filled her ears. Hers. It was followed by another moan as she angled her head to give Gabe greater access.

Her hand sought his jaw, and his short stubby whiskers tickled her fingertips. Truth be told, she'd imagined kissing Gabe and tracing her fingers along his jaw, more than once. That must account for her immediate and uninhibited surrender to him.

The next second, the assault intensified as Gabe slipped his tongue into her mouth. Reese didn't resist this either and melted farther into his embrace. His arms circled her, firm and strong, pulling her flush against him. She was trapped, exactly where she wanted to be.

The next low groan came from him, raw and desperate. Under different circumstances, Reese would have been thrilled with her ability to arouse this kind of excitement in him. Instead, the groan acted like a trigger and brought her to her senses. Their behavior was more than inappropriate. It was risky. Too much was at stake for her to make such a careless mistake.

Breaking off the kiss, she insisted, "We can't," in between short, shallow breaths. "Stop. Please."

He did. Sort of, in that he ceased kissing her. But he didn't move away and didn't give any indication he would. Lowering his head, he nuzzled the side of her face. The gesture was incredibly sensuous, sweetly tender and wildly romantic.

Who would have thought it? Gabe was an amazing kisser. With very little effort, he'd taken her to a place she'd never been before and might not ever go again. It was *that* good. And, she had to admit, her feelings for him were *that* strong.

"Gabe, we have to go inside." Sliding away from him, she all but leapt to her feet. This time, he let her go. Which was for the best because deep inside, she didn't want to leave the garage.

Rising casually—damn him for his composure; she was a basket case—he lifted the lid of the pine chest and retrieved the platter.

She hurried toward the door.

"Reese, hold up. We should go together. If not, my mom will think I did or said something to upset you." He paused, balancing the platter in the crook of his arm. The same arm he'd used to hold her tight moments ago. "Did I upset you?"

"No."

"Really? Because you look kind of flustered."

"I do?" She automatically smoothed her hair.

"Don't worry." He grinned. "You're gorgeous."

He'd been right the first time. She was flustered and more than a little mad at herself. She'd been wrong to encourage him.

"This is all my fault."

"I'm the one who kissed you."

"And I let you."

His grin widened. "Yeah, you did."

She rolled her eyes. He was such a guy. "Don't let it go to your head. I was simply curious."

"That wasn't the only reason you kissed me."

Of all the nerve! His confidence irritated

her. "Whatever the reason, it isn't going any further and won't happen again."

"Because of your job."

"Yes."

And because this was exactly the sort of rash behavior that had landed her in trouble twelve years ago with Blake. He'd been unavailable. Engaged to another woman. But Reese had fancied herself in love.

She would not be that person again. She'd grown up since then. Learned her lesson.

At least no one had seen her and Gabe or knew of their momentary indiscretion. As long as he didn't say anything, and he'd proved himself dependable when it came to keeping his mouth shut, they could forget all about the kiss.

Who was she kidding? She'd remember this kiss for the rest of her life. But she would try and pretend it hadn't happened.

"Come on." Gabe nodded in the direction of the door.

Reese didn't need to be asked twice. She flew through the door, raced across the laundry room and burst into the kitchen before coming to a sudden halt.

"There you are." Raquel stood with her hands upon her hips, and taking them in, a wide smile spread across her face. "Cara was about to go searching for you. We're almost ready to eat."

Four pairs of eyes fixed on them—Josh and Cole had come in from outside while Reese and Gabe were in the garage. Seeing the suspicion in all of their eyes, Reese was convinced she and Gabe had been busted.

Gabe presented his mother with the platter, his manner unconcerned. "It wasn't where I thought. We had to look around." He sauntered over to the counter. "Need me to carve the turkey?"

Reese snuck a peek at her hostess, feeling heat climb her neck and travel to her cheeks. This was going to be a long, awkward dinner.

Chapter 6

Gabe could sense Reese's embarrassment from the opposite side of the dining table. She spoke little, fidgeted a lot and ate hardly anything.

He probably shouldn't have kissed her. Okay, fine. He'd been out of line and taken advantage of her in a weak moment. But, damn, he'd do it again given half a chance.

The kiss had been electric. Phenomenal. If he hadn't been sitting on the chest, he'd have fallen to the garage floor. Who would have guessed? Him and Theo McGraw's daughter, kissing in the garage. If his father were alive, he'd disown Gabe.

Or would he? He had named Reese as trustee. Gabe still failed to grasp his father's reasoning. It must have been the chemo or pain medication muddling his brain.

Gabe couldn't use that excuse. Kissing her had been the furthest thing from his mind when they'd entered the garage. Then she'd told him about her daughter Celia. Thanked him for keeping her secret. Told him she trusted him and insisted he could trust her in return.

And what had he done? Abused that trust by kissing her. While she'd been a willing partner, he'd made the first move and elevated the kiss from a somewhat chaste, if not quite innocent, peck to a searing hot lip-lock.

It had been worth it. She'd shown him how good it could be between two people and how right it could feel.

"Gabe. Hey, Gabe. You listening?" Cara elbowed him in the side. "Josh asked you to pass the rice."

"Thanks," Josh said when Gabe roused himself from his stupor and handed over the large bowl.

"What's wrong?" Cara whispered.

"Nothing," Gabe insisted.

"I get it." She gave a tiny nod in the direction of his brothers, who were debating their favorite pie, pumpkin or apple. "I don't know what your mom was thinking, inviting them."

Gabe didn't correct Cara's assumption about his the reason for his distraction. "They *are* staying in the guest suite," he murmured.

"Yeah. Not to invite them would be rude. Too bad."

He ate mechanically, his gaze wandering the table. The next instant, Cara caught him staring at Reese.

"Well, well, well." A hint of amusement colored her voice.

"It's not what you think."

"You have no idea what I'm thinking."

"What are you two chatting about?" Gabe's mother asked, putting an immediate end to their private conversation.

"Nothing, Tia Raquel." Cara winked at Gabe.

He glanced away, not wanting to make Reese any more uncomfortable than she already was.

What was it about her that got to him? Before his father's illness, Gabe had dated. A couple of those former girlfriends had lasted long enough he'd considered making the relationship permanent. Considered, but hadn't acted on it. Something always held him back.

Until today, he hadn't realized what that was. Then he'd kissed Reese, and she had responded like no other. The incredible sparks were the missing component he'd been searching for.

"I was thinking," Josh said, "you could take me and Cole on a ride of the pasture lands tomorrow."

Gabe nearly choked on his bite of enchilada. "We're a little busy this week, vaccinating the calves and pregnancy checking the cows. I promised Violet I'd help her load the equipment and ready the vaccines."

"Cole and I will lend a hand."

At his mother's warning stare, Gabe ground his teeth together. "Be saddled up and ready to ride out at two."

Josh smiled, but Cole clenched his knife and fork as if attempting to bend them with his bare hands. "What about the morning?"

"Violet and I can handle it."

"If we're going to be partners on this ranch, Josh and I need to learn the ropes."

From anyone else, Gabe would have admired the man's persistence and determination. From Cole, it smacked of interference.

Again, his mother fired off a warning stare.

Again, Gabe reluctantly conceded. Damn the holidays and having to behave during dinner.

"We start at seven o'clock sharp."

"Breakfast is at six," his mother added sweetly. "In the summer, when it gets light out earlier, we eat at five-thirty."

Did she have to tell them everything?

"Thank you again for inviting me," Reese said during a pause. It was her first contribution to the conversation in a while and probably made to ease the tension.

"My pleasure." Gabe's mother beamed.

"Isn't it a little late in the season to vaccinate?" Cole asked.

The question startled Gabe. What did Cole know about raising cattle?

"Normally, we vaccinate in October. Time got away from us, what with Dad dying and all."

Gabe purposely refused to look at his mother, knowing she was annoyed at his snide tone. But, hell, his brothers had been eight hundred miles away while their mutual father wasted away during the final stages of colon cancer. Vaccinating calves and pregnancy checking cows had been the last thing on Gabe's and anyone's minds.

"Tortillas, anyone?" His mother held up a ceramic warmer.

Gabe suspected she was attempting to diffuse the tension.

"Yes, thank you," Reese answered, too brightly to be genuine.

Cara, Gabe's mother and Josh carried the conversation for the next several minutes, long enough for them to almost make it through dinner. Then the shit hit the fan when Cole opened his mouth.

"Cara, why is it you got one-sixth of the ranch?"

She drew back, startled. "I beg your pardon?"

"Aren't you just a family friend? "

"Cara is practically a member of this family," Gabe's mother said, rushing to Cara's defense. "And I'm sure August wanted to remember her. The work she does with the sanctuary is important. Those poor horses need someone to look out for them. They're neglected, starving and sometimes abused."

"But wouldn't the ranch benefit if you turned the sanctuary land over to the cattle?" Josh asked.

Josh's question hadn't come across as an attack like Cole's. Gabe was irritated nonetheless.

"The land belongs to Cara," he said. "She fosters over two hundred horses. We'd have to find somewhere to place them. That's a big job."

"I'm simply trying to figure this out." Josh's gaze traveled from Gabe to Cara, "Don't you want the ranch to get out of debt? We'd have a better chance with five hundred more acres. We wouldn't have to supplement the grazing land with grain and hay."

"It isn't our habit to discuss business at the table," Gabe's mother said firmly.

"Excuse me for saying, ma'am," Cole stressed the last word, "but we were discussing business a few minutes ago, and you didn't have a problem with it."

Gabe pushed back from the table, his chair scraping loudly across the hardwood floor. "What my mother means is we don't argue at the table. My father wouldn't allow it. But, then, you'd know that if you were ever here."

"For the record." Josh tossed his linen napkin onto the table. "Dear old Dad refused to let us come out for a visit. He told me so himself when I disobeyed my mother and called him fifteen years ago. He said I wasn't welcome."

Gabe's mother bit back a sob. "He always regretted that."

Josh's eyes flashed. "You're wrong, Raquel. He didn't have an ounce of regret. He couldn't have cared less about me or Cole."

"He loved you. It...it wasn't his fault." Her eyes filled with tears. "You don't understand."

"You're right." Cole ground out the words. "I don't understand a father who would turn his back on his children."

"The way I heard it, your mother left." Gabe could spar with the best of them and would be happy to oblige his brother.

Cole jumped to his feet. "Because of your mother."

Reese let out a small gasp.

"Stop it!" Cara cried out.

"I remind you," Gabe said stonily, "that you're staying in this house solely because of my mother's generosity."

Cole pointed at himself and Josh. "The house is two-thirds ours."

"She and Cara are entitled to remain here as long as they want."

"But the house doesn't belong to her, and she has no claim. She and our dad never married. Is that right?" He fired Reese a hostile look.

"I'm not an attorney," she said calmly. "My job is to carry out the terms of the will, not offer legal advice."

Gabe barely heard her. Cole's insinuations were another reminder Gabe wasn't legitimate. Was that the reason his father didn't leave him Dos Estrellas? Had he believed Josh and Cole would contest the will and try to take the ranch away from Gabe? As his legal offspring, they might have succeeded.

"My mother has been nothing but kind to you. Don't insult her."

Josh's face paled, and he and Cole walked away without excusing themselves.

"Good riddance," he said after them, then mumbled, "Greedy bastards."

Reese's eyes widened. Cara made a sound of disgust.

"What?" he demanded. "They are."

"Enough, *mijo*," his mother scolded in a tone Gabe hadn't heard since he was ten.

"They were ready to throw you from your home."

"Your brothers are our guests."

If he lived to be a hundred, he would never understand women.

"I owe you an apology," Gabe said.

"You've been doing that a lot lately." Reese hugged herself as if she might fly apart at the seams. "Apologizing."

"I had an outburst. Can you blame me?"

"You embarrassed your mother."

"They started it."

"Really, Gabe?"

Fresh anger surged, and he tried to tamp it down before he lost control again. "They were insulting and out of line."

"There's something to be said about taking the higher road."

"Right." He could hear his father making a similar remark when Gabe had punched Josh in the nose during their early school days. What would he have said back to his father if he'd known then what he knew now?

"It's Thanksgiving, Gabe. Holidays aren't a time for fighting with family."

"Can we save the lecture for another day?"

"You did ask me to stay."

"Sorry. Again."

She rolled her eyes.

Maybe he should quit while he was ahead and walk Reese to her car.

The two of them sat on the couch in the living room. She'd wanted to leave after the fiasco at dinner. Gabe had convinced her to remain and give him a chance to explain. Only he was doing a terrible job.

"It's been a difficult, weird day," she said.

"Not all of it." Gabe couldn't help smiling. "Parts of it were pretty darn good."

"Are you referring to…what happened in the garage?"

"We kissed, Reese. You can say it."

"Shh. Not so loud." She glanced worriedly around and whispered, "I thought we agreed to pretend that didn't happen."

"Speak for yourself. I, personally, am going to remember that kiss for a long time."

She closed her eyes and sighed.

"Okay, okay. I won't bring it up again." Today. He might want to talk about it again with her. Someday in the future, after he'd bought out his brothers' share of the ranch and was the sole owner. Then they'd be free to…what? Date? How would Reese feel about that?

"The argument between you and your brothers is the perfect example of why people choose a bank to be the trustee of their estate."

Gabe gave her a wry smile. "I'm beginning to see your point, much as I wish I didn't."

"Your father was a smart man."

"In some ways."

"No one's perfect."

"How's your father, by the way?"

She looked abruptly away. "Fine. Why?"

"His fall off the porch steps the other day. You left in a hurry."

"He's fine," she repeated. "Great."

"Glad to hear it."

She grabbed her purse on the floor beside her. "I should check on him."

"He'd call if he needed anything, right?"

"I suppose."

There was something off with her, more than the scene at dinner, and Gabe couldn't put his finger on it. She could feel guilty, he supposed, leaving her father alone on a holiday, even though she said he'd encouraged her to come.

"Speaking of fathers," Gabe said, "I remembered something the other day about mine that might interest you."

"Oh?"

"He liked you."

"You're kidding. We barely spoke." She seemed to relax.

"Well, I should say, he thought highly of you. He said it once. Admired you for going away."

"West Phoenix isn't exactly going away."

"You left the ranch and your father. That couldn't have been easy."

"I attended college. After Celia was born," she added in a quiet voice.

"But you didn't move back to Mustang Valley. Not for twelve years."

"There aren't many opportunities in a town this size for a person with a business degree. I was lucky to land the job at the bank. It was the first management position to open up there in four years."

"I think that's why Dad admired you. Because you chose a career you loved and didn't settle for being a rancher's daughter and marrying a local cowboy."

Her brows rose.

He might have been referring to himself, and she might have guessed.

"It's more than pursuing a career," she said. "I made a commitment to my cousin and her husband when they adopted Celia." Again, she lowered her voice. "I help with some of her expenses. Summer camp. Braces. Piano lessons. I also agreed to assist with her college education. I couldn't, won't, ask my father for that. Celia is my responsibility."

"That's very noble of you." He was sincere.

"I also like being my own person. I'm very independent."

Gabe nodded. "My dad was right to admire you."

She smiled, lighting up the room. "If he was still alive, I'd tell him thank you."

"Why *did* you come back to Mustang Valley?"

She stilled, taking her time to answer. "What's the old saying about coming home?"

"That's not an answer."

Reese ran her palms down the front of her jeans, then moved her purse to her other arm. "I should leave. It's getting late."

He'd pushed her too far and not for the first time today.

"Maybe someday you'll tell me what's going on." Gabe searched her face.

"Nothing's going on," she insisted and rose.

At the front door, he leaned down, intending to kiss her on the cheek.

"Gabe." She stepped back.

"If our fathers weren't rivals, and you didn't work for the bank, you and I would be friends. More than friends."

She laughed wryly. "I'm not sure about that."

Gabe was. "See you soon."

He walked back to the kitchen, a spring in his step. That was the closest to a normal, casual conversation he'd ever had with Reese. Truth be told, he rather liked it and could almost—*almost*—forget she'd turned down his request for a draw on the line of credit.

"Hey, you two," he asked his mother and Cara. "Need some help with the dishes?"

They turned from the sink and gave him the evil eye.

"I'm assuming you're mad about dinner."

"You have to ask?" Cara resumed loading the dishwasher.

"Reese gave me an earful earlier."

"I like her," his mother said over the running water.

"I'm sorry, Mom." He was tired of issuing apologies. "I didn't mean to ruin dinner."

"Your father wouldn't have wanted you to fight with your brothers."

"What would he have wanted, Mom? Because I sure as heck can't figure it out. Nothing makes any sense. He didn't care about his other sons until he got sick."

"You're wrong!" His mother shut off the water.

Cara grabbed a dishtowel and wiped her hands. "Why don't I leave you two alone so you can talk?" She didn't wait for an answer and left. He and his mother stood on opposite ends of the kitchen, each of them silently fuming. Gabe caved first. Sort of. What he did was ask the question he'd wanted answered all these years.

"Why didn't you and Dad ever marry?"

"He said once that he told you."

"Something about Abuelo not approving of him and you not going against your father's wishes."

"It's true."

"Seriously, Mom? You were an adult when you met Dad. If you'd wanted to marry him after he got his divorce, nothing Abuelo did or said could have stopped you."

"I don't want to talk about it."

"That's what you always say."

"You might think badly of your *abuelo*." She returned a pan to the cupboard.

"What did he do?" Gabe chuckled harshly. "Threaten you?"

She took a long time to answer. "Yes."

Gabe scowled. "With what? How?"

She sat at the table. Gabe did the same and gave his mother the moment she appeared to need in order to collect her thoughts.

"I promised your father I wouldn't ever tell you the details," she said with a sigh. "I suppose now it doesn't matter. Except..." She squeezed Gabe's hand, desperation shining in her eyes. "Please try and understand. Your *abuelo* did what he thought was best."

"Threatening someone is never best."

"Papi was raised in Mexico and didn't come to this country until he was a young man. His values and beliefs are those passed down to him from his father, and his father before him. Mexican men are revered as head of the household and their children, especially their daughters, obey them unconditionally. He is also very religious. Your father was separated when we met, staying temporarily with a friend, but still legally married."

Gabe hadn't heard that part of the story before. "He was separated?"

"He was intending to get a divorce. I was working in Scottsdale at a tree nursery. We met there."

Gabe had heard *that* part of the story.

"We started dating, fell in love and planned to marry. His wife, she changed her mind and convinced him to stay, using Josh as a reason. I was heartbroken, but didn't stop him. He had a son to think of." His mother paused. "He was gone a month before I realized I was pregnant with you. Hard as it was, I decided not to tell him."

"Dad didn't know about me." Gabe was stunned.

"Not until you were born. Someone at the nursery told him I was on maternity leave. Your father figured it out and insisted I move to Mustang Valley to be near him."

"And you did?"

"He told his wife he was getting a divorce. They weren't happy together. I wouldn't have moved here if I hadn't believed him."

"But was it true? They did have Cole after me."

"Yes. He had the papers drawn up when she told him she was pregnant."

"So, he stayed married, and you and he continued seeing each other." It was hard for Gabe to understand. His father had always preached honor and respect, yet he hadn't practiced those qualities. Not when it came to Gabe's mother.

"Eventually, your father did divorce. His wife left him and took their sons. My father still didn't approve. His religion doesn't favor divorce."

"You can't run your children's lives once they reach adulthood."

"My father ran mine," she admitted sadly. "He told me if I married your father, he would forbid me to have any contact with my mother and brothers."

"That's not only wrong, it's cruel." Gabe couldn't pick who he was madder at, his father or his grandfather. "What was he planning on doing? Ban you? Lock up Abuela and your brothers?"

"He would have forbidden them to see me, and Mama would not have disobeyed him."

"He's not in charge of—"

"You don't understand, *mijo*. You were raised by American parents. Mine have entirely different values. Your father understood and, for that reason, he refused to marry me. He didn't want to be responsible for cutting me off from my family. He'd already lost his sons."

"But Abuelo was all right with you two living together?"

"No, which is why they stayed at the inn in town and not at the house. But he believed a man has a responsibility to his children. He expected your father to raise and support you."

"He sounds like a hypocrite."

"Perhaps he is. But I respect him for his beliefs."

"Abuela would have found a way to see you and talk to you."

"Perhaps. And when Papi found out, he'd have made her life miserable. Your father wouldn't put her in that position. He did what he thought was best."

"For him. Not for you. Or me." Gabe hated how childish he sounded, but he'd suffered his entire life from his parents' decision not to marry and, it seemed, his grandfather's bullying tactics.

"Your father had a lot of regrets. One was you not getting the chance to know your brothers."

"He cut them off."

"He didn't."

"Are you going to tell me that was Abuelo's doing, too?"

"To a degree. Josh and Cole's mother was also responsible. She turned them against your father. Filled their heads with half-truths. Made him out to be a terrible person."

"Can you blame her for being angry? He had an affair." Gabe had loved his father always, but he was angry at him. "I was born in between Josh and Cole, which means he was sleeping with both her and you at the same time." At his mother's beet-red face,

Gabe felt ashamed. "I'm sorry, Mom. That was thoughtless of me."

"Try not to be so angry and bitter."

"It's hard to be anything but."

"Your father married because it was a good match, and he was of an age to settle down. Unfortunately, they were miserable together. When we met, it was like in the movies, fireworks exploding in the sky." She blushed anew. "We were wrong, I admit it. And our decisions caused a lot of hurt and pain for people we cared about. I would, however, do it again." She cupped Gabe's cheek. "Because I loved him more than life itself, and he gave me you."

"Why didn't he leave me the ranch like he promised?"

She returned her hand to her lap. "He was trying to make up to Josh and Cole for all the years he missed. And, I believe this with all my heart, he wanted to unite the three of you."

"Why didn't he try years ago?"

"He did. But, by then, the damage was done. Your brothers wanted nothing to do with him, and every overture he made was ignored or thrown back in his face."

Gabe was pretty sure if he looked up *dysfunctional family* in the dictionary, he'd read a description of the Dempseys and Salazars. If he wasn't so close to the situation, he'd laugh. Or get drunk. "Come on, Mom." He pushed back from the table. "I'll help you finish the dishes."

"You don't have to."

"The job will go faster with two people."

She smiled, relief in her expression, and chatted amiably about the upcoming Holly Daze Festival and the best time to haul out the Christmas decorations from storage.

Gabe understood that the causal banter helped take his mother's mind off her grief over his father's death and the unpleasant scene between him and his brothers. He wished he could say the same for himself.

Rather than feeling better, Gabe's anger and frustration continued to simmer. His mother had answered his question, but nothing had changed. He was still the illegitimate son who didn't inherit the ranch his father had promised him.

What an idiot he'd been earlier, thinking he could ask Reese out after this was all over. Without full ownership of the ranch and a respected place in the community, he had nothing to offer her. A woman like Reese deserved better.

Chapter 7

For the next week, Gabe grudgingly showed his brothers the ropes. Working together, they vaccinated the calves, checked the cows, offloaded the five semitruck loads of hay and conferred with the vet. Gabe was satisfied with the results. More cows were in condition to breed than last year. With luck, they'd increase the herd by a sizable amount.

If they could just hold out and keep the bill collectors at bay a while longer. Rain had yet to come to Mustang Valley, though the forecast was optimistic.

Wait a minute. *They*? He almost bit his tongue. He could not think of him and his brothers collectively. Whether they grew tired and eventually left, or he bought them out, they'd soon be gone.

He understood why Josh stayed. He needed a place he could bring his two children after the first of the year when he gained full custody of them. Cole, well, he remained a mystery.

The man had a decent rodeo career that he'd put on hold in order to stay at Dos Estrellas. Josh, too. Their mother's parents owned a horse ranch in Northern California where the brothers had been raised and learned to cowboy. Gabe had heard the two of them talking the other day, and their grandparents' place also served as their home base when they weren't on the circuit. Point being, Cole didn't have a compelling reason to remain in Mustang Valley.

The only reason Gabe could think of was his loyalty to Josh, something he'd observed on more than one occasion. It was an admirable quality, and his estimation of Cole was raised a small notch, not that he'd ever tell his younger brother.

He'd also never tell Cole how good he was with horses. And Josh was a quick learner who showed a knack for cattle management.

Had either of them been newly hired ranch hands, Gabe would credit them with potential. Because they stood between him and sole ownership of Dos Estrellas, he kept his mouth shut.

Gabe sat back in his father's office chair and stretched. Sitting at a desk and poring over papers wasn't his idea of a fun time. The past hour had dragged by like three. Neither Cole nor Josh had objected when Gabe stated he wanted to be the one in charge of record keeping. His motives had nothing to do with the fact that the task gave him an opportunity to talk to Reese almost daily.

She was patient with him and willing to answer his numerous questions. They'd covered balancing the monthly bank statements, updating income and expense spreadsheets, the liability insurance renewal and also a household budget. Gabe was learning a lot more about the business end of running a cattle operation than he'd thought possible.

One more thing the cancer had taken from him—Gabe's opportunity to learn this part of the family business from his father.

His anger from last week had dimmed, but the pain remained constant. How long until he stopped seeing his father's ghost everywhere in the house and barn?

His cell phone vibrated. Thinking it was the grain supplier, he was pleased to see Reese's name and number appear. This would be a nice break from the busy morning he'd had, crunching numbers and making calls.

"Hi, how you doing?" Funny, a month ago he couldn't have imagined himself happily answering a call from her. Neither could he have imagined kissing her. Yet, he'd done both and enjoyed it.

"We have a problem." She spoke in a rush.

"What's wrong?" His first thought was another unexpected bill. They'd received a whopper the other day, an overlooked co-pay balance from his father's specialist.

"Some of your cattle in section nine broke through the fence along the west line."

"Are they in with the Small Change livestock?"

"And some of ours are in with yours. Guess it's quite a mess up there, according to Enrico."

"I'll be right over." He shut off the ten-key calculator and desk lamp.

"Bring help," she said.

"That bad?"

"Apparently so."

The two neighbors had an unwritten agreement not to graze their cattle on adjacent land. Problem was, with the drought continuing, section nine had the best available grassland on Dos Estrellas. If Gabe and Violet hadn't moved a portion of their stock there, they'd be facing an even greater shortage of feed.

"Four-wheel, horseback or both?" Gabe asked.

"Both. We'll meet you there."

He assumed by *we* she meant her father, Enrico and any available Small Change hands.

"I'll call your father's cell when we're close." He had Theo McGraw's phone number, in case of an emergency, and Theo his.

"Call me," Reese told him.

"You're coming?"

"On my way now." She didn't wait for his response and disconnected.

Was she now? Gabe experienced a rush of anticipation. Passing his mother on his way out, he quickly filled her in on the problem and where he was going.

"Don't rush, I'll hold supper," she promised.

He kissed her cheek before racing from the

house to the horse stable, all the while mentally composing a to-do list. He'd send Violet and one of the hands by road in two of their four-wheel-drive quads. He'd go by horseback along with...

He spotted Cole, who'd been repairing a leak in the automatic watering system. Evidently, he was done, for he emerged from one of the stalls, toolbox in hand.

Gabe made a decision. "Where's Josh?"

"He's saddling up to ride out and tend the heifer with the skin lesions."

"Good. We're going in the same direction. You saddle up, too."

Cole's eyes widened. "What's wrong?"

For a fraction of a second, Gabe saw his father in Cole's face, and his gut tightened. It was less his features and more his expression.

How could that be? Cole had left the valley when he was five, never seeing their father again. Were things like expressions inherited?

Gabe cleared his throat. "We have a break in the fence on the west side of section nine. Our cattle are getting mixed in with those from the Small Change. I'm sending Violet by road. The three of us will ride out."

"I'll get Josh." Cole set the toolbox by the tack room door.

"Meet you at the gate."

Cole hurried off.

Gabe grabbed a halter from the tack room wall and headed straight to Bonita's stall. He'd need a horse with good cow sense for this job. Leading her to the hitching rail outside the tack room, he saddled and bridled her.

While he worked, he thought about Cole. His brother hadn't asked a lot of questions. Instead, he'd immediately set off in search of Josh. It was the kind of response Gabe would have expected from anyone who worked for him. The kind of response he'd expect from someone who understood the necessity of responding quickly in a crisis.

Okay, he'd give Cole credit for that, too. The real challenge, though, would come in an hour when they were separating the cattle and herding theirs back through the hole in the fence. He would see how well his brothers applied their rodeo skills to a real-life roundup.

Ten minutes later, the three of them were riding the back trail to section nine, the same trail he'd ridden the day he had found Reese trying to free her father's horse trapped in the sinkhole. In the distance, Violet and Joey, a young hand who'd started working for Dos

Estrellas this past summer, drove off in the Polaris quads. Twin plumes of dust rose from the rear wheels.

Before leaving, Violet had loaded the necessary tools and materials for repairing the fence into a crate strapped to the back of her quad. Maintaining the condition of the fences was her job, and Gabe had heard her disappointment with herself when they talked.

Once they arrived in section nine, separating the cattle wouldn't be hard. Each one was marked with an identifying ear tag. In case there was a question, Violet carried the log with her.

The actual rounding up of the cattle would be done with both vehicles and horses. The quads could cover more ground at a faster rate while the horses could turn on a dime and maneuver in between cattle, cutting one out from the group and moving it in the desired direction.

If all went well, they'd be done by dark, three hours from now, and Gabe would be twenty minutes late for dinner at most. His brothers, too, as his mother insisted they share meals together despite the continued awkwardness.

"How far is it?" Josh asked. He kept pace easily with Gabe.

"Two miles."

They pushed their horses along, alternating between a fast walk and a trot, depending on the terrain. They didn't lope, not wanting to tire out their mounts. The wind increased the farther away from the ranch they traveled, making Gabe appreciate his heavy coat. Cole lifted the collar around his neck and fastened the snap.

Talk was at a minimum. Over the next rise, they reached the boundary of section six, part of the land designated to Cara's mustang sanctuary.

A herd of orphaned yearlings, grazing peacefully a half mile away, raised their heads and whinnied. The next instant, they galloped eagerly toward Gabe and his brothers. Over a dozen in all, they formed a small stampede, coming to a lumbering halt and walking the last hundred yards to the fence where they stood bunched together, staring.

Neither Josh's nor Cole's horses reacted much, which was a good sign. They might indeed do well with the cattle despite seldom being ridden outside the rodeo arena.

Gabe and his brothers arrived at section nine. Violet and Joey had beaten them to the site of the broken fence, along with Reese, Enrico and two other hands from the Small Change. Theo McGraw, Gabe noticed, was absent. Strange. The man diligently watched the goings-on at his ranch like a hungry hawk.

About twenty head of cattle were being kept clustered together on the Dos Estrellas side of the fence. Twice that many were on the Small Change side. Violet threaded her way through the nervous cattle on foot, verifying the ear tags. She spotted Gabe and motioned to him.

He waved in return, but didn't ride over. He had seen Reese. She sat astride her father's horse, wind tossing the hair peeking out from beneath her cowboy hat.

She made a striking picture, and Gabe wanted a closer look. To get there, he had to ride through the hole in the fence. Violet hailed him before he made it.

"Gabe, we have a couple injured heifers here. You should have a look."

Work came first, he thought with more than a little disappointment and reluctantly turned Bonita around.

Gabe and Cole pushed the last Dos Estrellas calf through the hole in the fence and onto ranch property. Bawling loudly, the calf ran to join its mother and the rest of the herd meandering down the hillside and the long stretch of flat land ahead. In just over two hours they'd finished dividing the cattle and treating the two heifers with nasty lacerations on their legs. His brothers had performed well, demonstrating skill and taking instruction without complaint.

They weren't the only ones. Reese, too, had done her share. She was a competent horsewoman, and years away from her father's ranch hadn't affected her abilities. She was Theo McGraw's daughter, all right. Born into the life.

Except, she hadn't chosen it and, instead, worked in a bank, which also suited her.

Watching her dismount and help Violet with the fence repair, he decided he liked her better in jeans and boots than slacks and dress shoes, though she certainly wore the business attire well. Maybe he liked her in anything.

"Gabe, can you lend us a hand?" Violet shouted. She and Reese were struggling with the posthole digger.

He was more than happy to oblige and pushed Bonita ahead, ignoring Josh's questioning look and Cole's dubious one. Dismounting, he dropped the reins to the ground, confident Bonita would stand obediently. She didn't disappoint him and, lowering her head, nuzzled at the sparse tufts of grass.

Therein was the problem. If not for grass being in short supply, the cattle wouldn't have gone searching for, as the saying went, greener pastures.

He would need to talk to his brothers about supplemental feed. And soon.

Reese handed the posthole digger to Gabe. Their gazes connected briefly, and a lovely smile touched her lips, mesmerizing him and reminding him of Thanksgiving when he'd tasted—

Reluctantly, he looked away. He didn't allow his eyes to linger, not with Violet standing right there. His livestock foreman wasn't blind or stupid.

Holding the posthole digger with both hands, he raised it level with his head, then drove it forcefully into the ground. The shovel blades hit with a solid *thunk*. Squeezing the two handles together, he lifted the posthole digger and deposited the dirt into a nearby pile started by Violet and Reese.

They'd been right to request his help; the ground was dry and hard.

"I heard from Banner Hay Sales today," Reese said. "One of their clients backed out, leaving them with ten semitrucks of hay for sale. They offered me a deal."

She named the price, and Gabe paused momentarily in his digging. Winter was a bad time of year to buy hay, prices were typically high. While still costly, the price Reese quoted was good. Better than good. And wasn't he thinking of talking to his brothers about supplemental feed?

"We can't afford ten trucks."

Thwank! The sound the shovel blades made when they hit the ground echoed inside Gabe's chest.

"I thought we could split the purchase," Reese said. "Five trucks each."

He sensed Violet's impatience. She knew how important it was they have enough feed to survive the winter. Five truckloads wouldn't last them through more than a couple of weeks, but it might make all the difference.

Thwank! Another shovelful of dirt was added to the growing pile.

"We'd have to borrow from the line of credit."

"Yes." Reese adjusted her leather gloves.

"You'd approve the draw?"

"I wouldn't have mentioned the hay purchase otherwise."

Gabe slammed the posthole digger into the ground again, with such force, the shovel blades clanged loudly.

Reese was doing her job, seeing to the financial security of Dos Estrellas, of which the line of credit was a part. Yet, it galled Gabe. She wouldn't give him the money for buying more cattle, a practically guaranteed way of growing the herd. She would, however, authorize a draw to purchase hay, something that was her idea.

"How long do I have to decide?" he asked.

Confusion flashed in her eyes. She had assumed he'd readily agree. "Banner gave us until tomorrow. They have other buyers," she added.

Her comment struck Gabe as a threat rather than an incentive. If he were to decline, Dos Estrellas alone would suffer. The Small Change could easily afford five truckloads of hay. They could afford all ten trucks.

Violet's stare burned into Gabe.

"I'll let you know," he said.

"We can't wait," Reese protested.

Thwank! "You said I have until tomorrow."

She expelled a long breath. "Fine. Ten o'clock is our deadline. You should probably discuss this with your brothers."

That irked Gabe more than her blatant power struggle. Without a word, he handed Violet the posthole digger, which she carried to the quad and secured to the crate with a pair of bungee cords.

"We don't have to do this," Reese told Gabe when they were alone.

"Do what?"

"Fight."

"I'm not fighting with you."

"Proving who's in charge, then."

"You said it. Not me."

She groaned. "Think about what your father would have done. We both know he'd buy the hay."

"And you can predict his behavior because the two of you were so close."

"I told you before, I barely spoke to him. But I did live next door to him for years and listened to my father talk about him all my life. Your father was smart, and he put the herd first. The entire ranch."

Gabe didn't need a talking-to. Not from Reese and not with their employees and his brothers in the nearby vicinity. He knew buying the hay was a good decision. And if he'd used the line of credit to purchase additional cattle, the hay would have depleted the line faster. What he resented was Reese calling the shots *and* reminding him he had to confer with his brothers. *He* should be the one making the decisions. No one else.

Picking up the fence post, he slammed it into the hole he'd dug. "Hold this," he ordered.

Reese grabbed the top of the post and kept it steady while he filled the opening with dirt and packed it down. By the time he finished, Violet had returned. Using a pair of pliers, she reattached the barbed wire to the post. When the fence was secure, Gabe started for his horse.

Reese appeared beside him. "Gabe."

"Is there something else?"

She hesitated, peering over his shoulder as if making sure they weren't being overheard. "I don't want it to be like this between us."

"You can't have it both ways." He didn't slow his pace to accommodate her shorter strides. "We're either friends—more than friends—or you're the trustee of my father's estate and the one running Dos Estrellas."

"Not running the ranch. I simply oversee the finances."

"There's a fine line. Especially since you're the one authorizing the purchases."

"We need to get along."

"Then quit kissing me," he snapped.

"You made the first move!"

"You're right. My fault."

"No, it isn't."

Several seconds passed, silent except for the sound of her soft panting and the crunch of their boots on the rocky ground.

She gave in first. "Don't let your personal feelings regarding me interfere with you making the best decision for the ranch."

"I'll call you tomorrow." Gabe reached Bonita's side. The mare hadn't moved but a few feet. Patting her neck, he lifted the reins over her head and mounted.

Gabe rode off with his brothers, following in the wake of Violet and Joey on the quads. His last sight was of Enrico joining Reese before he helped her crawl through the fence and onto Small Change land.

"You two have a fight?" Cole asked. He sat easy in the saddle, not showing the least sign of fatigue despite putting in a full day. Josh, neither.

They were good workers. Gabe would give them that.

"Banner Hay Sales has ten semitruck loads of hay for sale at a fair price," he said, hating he was doing exactly as Reese had suggested. "Reese will authorize a draw from the line of credit if we want to buy it."

We. There it was again.

"Aren't we going to need hay?" Josh asked matter-of-factly. He clearly hadn't let Reese's position as trustee get under his skin.

They rode three abreast down the hillside. In the distance, the cattle they'd driven from the Small Change grazed on the sparse grass. By nightfall, they would join the main herd.

"Yeah, we'll need it," Gabe agreed with his brother.

"You tell her yes?"

"Said I'd—we'd—decide and call her in the morning."

"Why wait?"

Gabe pulled his horse up short. His brothers did the same.

"If we buy the hay, we're going to have to commit to maintaining the herd through the winter." Like their father's plan called for. "Find a means to purchase more supplemental hay. Not sell off stock."

"Didn't we already decide?" Josh asked.

"It's another debt. We'd have to make monthly interest payments."

"What's the weather forecast?" Cole asked.

"No rain for at least two weeks."

"Then we don't have a choice."

Cole's sudden change of heart made Gabe wary. "All you want is to sell the ranch."

"You and Josh won't agree to that, which leaves me stuck here."

"Not a good enough answer."

"What do you want from me?" Cole's voice carried an unmistakable edge.

"One year." Gabe couldn't quite believe what he was saying. All he'd wanted since his brothers first arrived at Mustang Valley was for them to leave. "We agree right here and now to give it our best effort. Grow the herd and pay off as many of Dad's medical bills as we can. Plus the interest on the line of credit. At the end of one year, we can discuss selling the ranch."

"You'd agree to sell?" Cole eyed him suspiciously.

"Yes."

"And if we aren't in a position to sell?"

"We will be, as long as we work our tails off."

Cole looked to Josh, and his brother nodded. "All right. One year."

Gabe held out his hand to Cole, who shook it. He then did the same with Josh.

"How 'bout that." Cole grinned.

No doubt he was happy. He saw himself getting a bundle for his share of the ranch at the end of a year. Josh, too, would have more than enough to take care of his children.

Gabe pushed Bonita ahead. He was okay with his brothers believing they were going to get out from under the burden of Dos Estrellas. In reality, he had every intention of being that buyer for the ranch and much sooner than a year. To accomplish his goal, he'd need to play by Reese's rules.

The thought left a bad taste in his mouth.

Chapter 8

Gabe dragged the last box of Christmas lights across the attic floor to the edge of the opening. He carefully lowered himself down the ladder one step at a time. When his shoulders were level with the opening, he grabbed the box of lights and carried them down to the garage floor.

Thank goodness this was a once-a-year job. Twice a year, if he counted a month from now when he'd be carting the half dozen boxes of lights back up to the attic.

His mother was getting a head start this year. Thanksgiving was just ten days ago. Usually, she waited until closer to Christmas to start decorating the house. Not decorating last year—his father had been too sick—made her want to go all-out this season.

He carried the box of lights to the front courtyard, and deposited it next to the others. "That's it, Mom."

She and Cara were bundled up from head to toe, as the weather had taken a turn. Colder, but not wetter. There was still no sign of rain. With their striped stocking caps, scarves and mittens, they resembled a pair of Christmas elves.

Gabe wished he were like them and more in the spirit of the season. He was anything but jolly. His mood hadn't gone unnoticed, and his mother was constantly trying to cheer him. Yesterday, she'd baked his favorite dessert. Double-layer chocolate cake. The day before, she'd made turkey soup with the Thanksgiving leftovers and mended his favorite shirt.

He suspected her motives weren't entirely selfless. She had her own troubles. She missed his father and worried about losing her home. Cooking and decorating kept her busy. This would be her first holiday in thirty years without August. Also, she missed her parents, who'd announced they wouldn't be visiting until the spring. Make that, his *abuelo* had announced it during their last phone conversation. Gabe doubted his *abuela* had much say in the matter.

"Can you help with this?" Cara asked. "I'm too short."

She was standing on a stepladder, attempting to hang a string of lights on the peaked eve above the front door.

Gabe didn't ask how she'd managed to hang the rest of the lights while he'd been going back and forth between the attic and the courtyard, carrying boxes.

"Let me," he pretended to grouse. "You're going to hurt yourself."

Cara relinquished the stepladder. Gabe's mother came over to supervise.

"It's drooping too much," she commented when Gabe attached the lights.

He grunted, but obligingly restrung the section of lights to hang evenly. For the next thirty minutes Gabe toiled, until his shoulders and back began to ache.

Cara handed him a red bulb. "There are too many blue ones on that string."

"I have better things to do on a Saturday afternoon than take this abuse." He thought of the hundred and one chores waiting for him. "The water troughs in the horse pastures need scrubbing."

"Everyone deserves a day of rest now and then," his mother said.

"Hanging Christmas lights isn't a day of rest."

"The troughs can wait until tomorrow. Josh and Cole went into town. Sightseeing, they said."

What was to see in Mustang Valley? he mused. The small community had only a diner, a halfway-decent market, one gas station and a couple of bars—

That was it. They were probably going to the Poco Dinero Saloon and Grill. Sightseeing his foot! As kind as Gabe's mother had been to them, they should be the ones helping her string these stupid lights.

"I promise, I'll make it worth your while." His mother smiled up at him. "Roast beef for dinner."

She might be cooking day and night in an effort to keep herself busy, but Gabe was reaping the benefits.

"Fine," he grumbled and plugged in the next string of lights.

They'd mostly finished when his mother called it quits. "That's enough for today."

Good. Gabe was starving.

She didn't make him wait long, and a half hour later, the three of them sat at the kitchen table, eating dinner. The roast beef was delicious.

"*Mijo*, do you have any plans tonight?"

He was contemplating crashing early. Quite the life of a bachelor. Pretty pathetic, actually. His brothers were still out, whooping it up, he assumed. Well, more chocolate cake for him.

"Nothing much." Gabe shoveled another bite into his mouth.

"Cara and I were thinking…"

Uh-oh. He recognized that tone and readied himself to say no. Whatever his mother had in mind, he wouldn't like it.

"I'm kind of tired, Mom."

"The Holly Daze Festival started last night." She sent Cara a conspiratorial look.

"Your mom would like to go," Cara said.

"Okay. Go." He'd get the TV to himself. Maybe watch the Phoenix Suns play and have a beer.

"She wants you to take her."

Gabe looked up from his plate. "Why me?"

"You should get out of the house," his mom said.

"I hate to disappoint you, Mom. But if I was

inclined to get out of the house, it wouldn't be to attend the Holly Daze Festival."

"They added a new arts and crafts display. I hear there's a lot of great gifts for sale."

"I don't know." He did know—he'd rather stick sharp needles in his eyes than go to an arts and crafts display. "You can't drive yourself?"

"That truck is a pain."

Manual transmission. His mother had never mastered the technique. "What about Cara? Can't you ride with her?"

"I have to go early to help with the raffle booth."

He vaguely remembered her saying something about volunteering.

"Please, *mijo*," his mother implored.

"I'll drop you off. Call me when you're ready to be picked up."

"Won't you stay? The Powells will be there."

"They're running the booth with me," Cara said. "We're selling raffling tickets for carriage rides. The proceeds go to the mustang sanctuary. You know how much we need the money."

"We'll see."

"Thank you." His mother smiled as if he'd agreed.

Gabe did like the Powells, one of the more prominent families in Mustang Valley. Unlike Theo McGraw, they weren't in competition with Dos Estrellas. The Powells owned and operated a horse ranch and riding stable.

They were also responsible for Cara's mustang sanctuary. A few years ago, they'd captured Prince, the last wild mustang in the valley, and rehabilitated him. The stallion was now their prized stud horse and, between stud fees and selling his offspring, responsible for bringing Powell Ranch back from the edge of bankruptcy.

Gabe's family could use their own lucky discovery, like a pot of gold at the end of the rainbow. But rain was required for a rainbow, and there didn't seem to be any in sight.

The Powells had taken in refugee mustangs after Prince, most of them coming from other parts of the state. Cara, friends with the Powell brothers' wives, had helped. Cara was a talented horsewoman and had worked wonders with several incorrigible rebels in the past. Eventually, she brought a few mustangs to Dos Estrellas.

After her son died, she brought more and

more mustangs to Dos Estrellas. No one complained, understanding she needed an outlet for her grief. Eventually, she took over the entire sanctuary, which was then moved from Powell Ranch to Dos Estrellas. Cara kept the mustangs she couldn't find good homes for. None were ever turned away.

When Gabe and his mother arrived at the Holly Daze Festival, he got out of the truck rather than go home.

The arts and crafts tables were on the north side of the square, which was illuminated from end to end with colorful lights. A fifteen-foot Christmas tree towered in the center, though it wasn't yet decorated. That community tradition took place next weekend with people encouraged to bring their own ornaments.

Gabe looked around. The Poco Dinero Saloon and Grill wasn't a far walk, across the street and up a block. His brothers might still be there. If not, there'd likely be a buddy or two with whom he could waste the next couple of hours.

There would also be members of the fairer sex. If Gabe was in the market, he could possibly coerce one of them into a dance.

It was an idea that should appeal to him and

used to greatly. Instead, his mind was centered on one particular woman. Reese.

"Aren't you going to buy a raffle ticket?" his mother asked. "There's a drawing every hour."

"Who would I take on the carriage ride if I won?"

"You're missing the point." She steered him toward the booth where Cara and the Powells sat.

"Don't we already donate enough?"

"*Mijo.*"

"Fine. One ticket."

At the booth, Cara greeted them with a huge smile. He hadn't seen her that enthused in a long while and wound up buying two tickets.

"Thank you," Caitlin Powell said brightly when he handed over his ten-dollar bill. She was married to Ethan, the middle Powell brother. "Good luck."

Gabe had half a mind to tear up the tickets or give them to the nearest person. But, distracted by an acquaintance, he jammed the tickets into his coat pocket.

Five minutes later, he bid his acquaintance Merry Christmas and strolled in the direction of the saloon. A moment later, he came to an abrupt halt. There, not thirty feet in front of him, stood Reese.

The sight of her wasn't what glued his boots to the cement sidewalk. It was his brother Josh and the two of them conversing easily, as if they were old friends.

No, more than friends. Gabe wasn't born yesterday. He recognized the look of a man interested in a woman, and Josh had that look.

Why should he care? Gabe had no claim on Reese. She could talk to whomever she wanted. Except the burning sensation in his gut propelled him forward until he was literally upon them.

Startled, Reese turned wide eyes on him. "Gabe, what are you doing here?"

The loudspeaker attached to a nearby post crackled to life.

"Attention, attention. The winner of this hour's drawing for the carriage ride is ticket number 23853, Gabe Dempsey. Gabe, will you and your party please report to the carriage station at the south end of the square."

He took Reese's hand. "Come on."

"What!" She tried to pull away.

"You're my party. For the carriage ride."

"I happen to be talking to Josh, in case you didn't notice."

He glared at his brother. "You don't mind, do you?"

Josh chuckled. "Not at all. Have fun, you two."

"Thanks." Gabe dragged Reese down the sidewalk, ignoring her protests.

She should be mad. What right did Gabe have to tear her away from a perfectly cordial conversation with Josh to…what? A carriage ride? Of all the nerve! Could his me-Tarzan-you-Jane attitude be more annoying?

She *should* be mad. Secretly, Reese was pleased. Kind of giddy. And flattered.

"Can we go a little slower?" she pleaded.

Gabe reduced his speed by a fraction.

"What's with you?"

"We have to hurry."

"The carriage isn't going anywhere." Her words had no effect on him or how fast he walked. "Why, Gabe? Don't tell me you're jealous."

That made him slow down, then stop. "Of Josh?"

"He is the person I was talking to."

"No way."

"Then, care to explain this race we're on?"

"I can't."

"Because?"

"I'm not sure why." He started walking again, a frown darkening his features. She should pull away, but she rather liked the sensation of his strong, warm fingers wrapped firmly around hers. In some ways, it was more intimate than when they'd kissed, though not as enjoyable.

"Ask me." She struggled to keep pace, hampered by her knee-high, spike-heeled boots.

"Ask you what?"

"To go with you on the carriage ride. I'd like to be invited. Not forced."

He let go of her hand, making her regret her words. The loss of intimacy was that keen. "And what will you answer?"

"You won't know unless you—"

He caught her by the arms. People passed them on both sides. Reese barely noticed. She saw only Gabe. His eyes, seeming to take in every aspect of her face, and the five-o'clock shadow covering his jaw. It gave his appearance a dangerous and wildly sexy edge.

"Would you like to go on the carriage ride with me?"

For a guy who looked good enough to devour, the blandly delivered line was a letdown. Middle school kids selling candy for their fund-raisers had better pitches. She thought of telling him no. He deserved it after his ridiculous behavior.

"I would," she said. "Very much."

"Good," he grunted and resumed dragging her along.

At least he was holding her hand again.

Ethan Powell waited by the horse-drawn carriage parked alongside the curb. With his cowboy hat, jeans, jacket and boots, he didn't look much like a carriage driver, but the carriage itself was right out of a fairytale. Illumination from the streetlight added to the magical illusion.

Reese caught her breath. "How pretty."

"I guess."

She rolled her eyes at Gabe's remark, then returned her attention to the carriage, committing the lovely sight to memory. A snowwhite lacquer exterior set off the red velvet upholstered seats. Large-spoked rear wheels contrasted the much smaller front ones. Brass lanterns attached to the sides glowed a soft golden yellow. Even the horses, a matching pair of blacks with shiny silver accent trim on their bridles, were perfect.

"You're the lucky winner?" Ethan Powell

pushed off from where he leaned against the carriage and sent them an amused smile.

"Gabe is. I'm his party." Reese ran her hand along the side of the carriage's gleaming exterior.

She'd been raised around horses. Her father had taught her to ride by the time she was three. But, like many little girls, she'd dreamed of being a princess. This carriage ride was probably as close as she'd ever get to realizing that dream.

"Thank you, Gabe." She sighed wistfully.

"Sure."

He didn't understand. He was a man, after all. Besides, it wasn't necessary. She'd enjoy every moment of the ride regardless.

Ethan opened the small door built into the side of the carriage and extended his hand. "Climb aboard."

She placed her foot on the narrow step. Ethan held her elbow, helping her up. The carriage rocked gently as she settled into the far side of the seat. Her hand brushed the velvet upholstery. The carriage rocked harder as Gabe climbed in and plunked down beside her.

He didn't appear concerned with the upholstery or anything else about the carriage, including her. Rather, he stared off toward the festival.

"You may need this." Ethan handed them a thick, fluffy blanket. "It's going to get cold."

He was right. Reese could well imagine the drop in temperature once they were moving. She took the blanket and spread it out across her and Gabe's laps.

"Cozy," he said.

His tone perplexed her. Was he being funny or serious? A glance at his profile offered no answers.

"All set?" Ethan asked.

Reese nodded, afraid if she spoke, she'd sound exactly like the excited little-girl-wan-nabe-princess coming to life inside her.

The driver's seat, situated in front, was considerably higher than where Reese and Gabe sat in the back. Ethan hauled himself up effortlessly—not an easy feat with a pros-thetic leg. He'd lost his when he'd served in the Marines. He untied the reins from the brake handle, released the brake and clucked to the horses. The carriage lurched and they were off, the horses' iron shoes clip-clopping loudly on the blacktop.

Reese was instantly captivated. She'd seen the community of Mustang Valley thousands of times. She could probably travel the length of it blindfolded. But never had she seen it by carriage. The storefronts looked more charming, less stark and businesslike. The Christmas lights and tree in the center of town might have come straight from Santa's Village. The people, too, were different, smiling and waving gaily as they passed.

As the minutes flew by, Reese's heart soared higher and higher. Sitting with Gabe, snuggled beneath the blanket, increased her happiness. The ride couldn't be more romantic, and she thought of asking him how he truly felt about her.

"The hay was delivered the other day," he said.

Reese blinked. Really? A romantic carriage ride and he wanted to talk shop?

"It looks good," he added. "High quality. You were right to suggest purchasing it."

"I don't want to discuss the hay," she snapped, then bit her lip.

"Okay." Gabe resumed staring at the passing sights.

She suppressed a groan. He was either being intentionally obtuse or didn't get the hint. She decided to go out on a limb.

"If you and I weren't at odds—"

"We're not at odds."

"Weren't in a work relationship, then." She infused warmth into her voice. "This carriage ride might be going quite differently."

"How so?"

"For starters, you'd be looking at me and not the big sale sign in front of Valley Auto Parts."

He turned to face her. "I thought you wanted to keep our relationship strictly professional."

"I do." She should. "Just making small talk."

"So was I when I mentioned the hay."

Touché.

Several more minutes passed in silence.

At the next corner, Ethan pulled the horses to a stop and peered over his shoulder at Reese and Gabe. "You have a preference for which route we take?"

"No." Reese said.

"Hickory Street," Gabe countered.

She blinked in surprise. Hickory Street would take them to the outskirts of town. It would be dark there. No streetlights. And more isolated. Also…dare she think it?…romantic. But hadn't Gabe recently reminded her of their agreed-upon terms? Strictly professional.

"You got it," Ethan said and clucked to the horses.

With another lurch, they continued on, the horses resuming their slow, steady trot. Two blocks passed, then three.

"You guys are awfully quiet," Ethan said, this time without looking at them.

"Taking in the scenery," Reese answered, and she was. The distant mountains were blue-black against a star-filled sky. To the right of the rounded peaks, the lights of Scottsdale glittered, appearing much closer than the actual thirty miles away as the crow flies.

"Yeah, taking in the scenery," Gabe echoed. Reese started at the feel of his breath on the back of her neck and the silky timbre of his voice. She turned in the seat and gasped softly when she found him mere inches away. Close enough to...

"Oh, my."

"You're prettier now than you were in school." His low whisper ignited a flurry of sparks in the place his breath had moments ago caressed. They quickly spread, making her both nervous and excited.

"Gabe. We have an agreement."

"I was never very good at following rules." He skimmed his fingers along the curve of her cheek. "And breaking them with you is very tempting."

She closed her eyes, savoring the moment. "This is a bad idea."

"It's the best one I've had since Thanksgiving."

"I thought you were mad at me about the hay."

"Didn't I admit you were right?"

She pressed her palm to his cheek. "Your father just died. You're at odds with your brothers. The ranch is in debt. The timing couldn't be worse."

"I'm going to kiss you, Reese."

The sparks ignited a shiver. "You say that like I don't have a choice."

"You do. You can tell me no. But I happen to think you'd like me to kiss you, too."

He was obviously skilled at mind reading. "What about Ethan?" She shot their driver a concerned glance.

"Trust me, he's not paying us any attention."

Gabe's confidence was annoying. It was also very attractive. She was falling for him in a way she hadn't fallen for a man before. It was a little scary.

He lowered his head. Their mouths were almost, nearly, and then barely touching. "What do you want from me?" she whispered.

"Surrender."

That was all the encouragement Reese needed. The last barrier vanished, and she was in his arms, kissing him as if this moment were the one she'd been waiting for her entire life. Heedless, mindless and careless, she did as he wanted and gave in to him. It was glorious.

He drew her into the circle of his arms, flush with his hard, unyielding chest while his mouth played hers like a fine instrument. The motion of the carriage elevated the sensations. If Reese let her mind wander, she and Gabe could be floating adrift on a vast ocean, all alone, their problems nonexistent.

Nice, but not very realistic. Nonetheless, she reveled in their kiss. What would one more minute hurt?

There must have been a pothole in the road, for the carriage bumped hard, knocking them both sideways and breaking off the kiss.

Instead of coming to her senses, being embarrassed or chiding herself for her reckless behavior, Reese laughed.

"That's better." Gabe adjusted the blanket,

which had slipped from their laps. "I like you when you're happy."

"When am I not happy?" The question was no sooner expressed then she remembered. The night of their prom. Her mood shifted, and she extracted herself from his arms. "We should probably…"

"Yeah."

She heard his reluctance as clearly as if he'd spoken it. "It won't always be like this. A lot could change in a year." Josh, not Gabe, had mentioned the brothers' agreement to work together.

"Nothing about our families will change. You'll always be Theo McGraw's daughter, and I'm the product of August Dempsey's affair with my mother."

"We don't have to let our past define us."

He smiled tenderly. "I didn't realize you were such an optimist."

"Be patient."

"What choice do I have?" His smile changed from tender to sad.

She suspected few people saw this side of him and was glad he felt comfortable enough with her to let down his guard.

"Next stop, the center of town." Ethan pulled on the reins, slowing the horses, who'd picked up the pace when they realized the ride was nearing an end. Ahead, the lights of the square blinked brightly.

Reese couldn't believe where the minutes had gone. She and Gabe had been completely absorbed—with their kiss and each other.

Unfortunately, none of her uncertainties had been assuaged. She still had no clue where their relationship was heading.

She didn't like that. Reese always strove to maintain perfect order. Even when the rug was pulled out from under her, like getting pregnant, she found a solution and acted promptly. But when it came to her and Gabe, she had no solution. No expectations. No promises. It was scary—and thrilling.

Gabe's fingertips linking briefly with hers when she exited the carriage implied they shared a secret.

Another one.

Chapter 9

Finding a reason to go home at lunch was becoming a habit for Reese. For the fourth day in a row, she was making the fifteen-minute trek from the bank, this time with her father's prescription in her purse. He didn't need it until tonight and would most likely see through her excuse.

Big deal. If he objected, then they could hire a caretaker.

Seconds before Reese reached the Small Change, she saw a familiar-looking vehicle pull out. Her suspicions were confirmed when she and the truck passed on the road, and she got a good look at the driver.

Cole Dempsey! What was he doing here? Who had he seen? Did her father know?

Reese rushed inside the moment after she parked in the garage. "Dad, you here?"

There was no answer. Maybe her father was in the barn or at one of the livestock pens. He did venture outside at least once a day when he was feeling his best.

"Dad. Dad!"

"In here." His voice came from the TV den.

Reese breathed a long sigh of relief and dropped her purse onto the kitchen counter, along with the prescription. Her father was sitting in his favorite recliner, fiddling with the remote. "How you doing?" She was anxious to know about Cole Dempsey but unsure if she should ask. If Cole had been talking to Enrico or one of the hands, she'd prefer to grill them first, without her father's knowledge.

"I had a visitor." Her father wore a satisfied expression.

Aha.

"Who?" Reese asked, pretending ignorance.

"Cole Dempsey." He set down the remote. "Kid's the spitting image of his mother. You probably don't remember her."

"No." Reese decided to be blunt. "Why was he here?"

"Paying me a neighborly visit."

She knew better than that. "Come on, Dad."

"He's interested in selling his share of Dos Estrellas."

"You're kidding." Reese's knees weakened a little. She wobbled to the sofa and sat. "He offered it to you?"

"Yep." Her father leaned back in the recliner and pushed on the side handle, raising the foot rest.

Her father must be having a good day. With his tremors and loss of strength, he couldn't always manage his recliner.

"Did he happen to mention if his brothers knew?"

"What does it matter?"

"They're partners, Dad. It matters a lot."

"Is he prohibited from selling without their consent?"

"No. Consent is needed only for selling the entire ranch." Reese had found that part of the living trust unusual and interesting. Anyone could wind up owning a share of Dos Estrellas and partnering with the remaining brother or brothers, including, possibly, a rival. August Dempsey must have thought of that. He'd paid meticulous attention to every other detail.

Could it have been intentional? A test for his sons? She wouldn't put it past August. But, if true, he'd taken an incredible risk that could easily backfire.

Hearing her father's jovial chuckle, she was angry. "You can't seriously be considering accepting Cole's offer."

Deep furrows creased his brow. "I am. Why wouldn't I?"

"We've had this discussion before. Running the Small Change is hard enough. You're in no—" She'd started to say shape, but changed her mind. "No position to take on more responsibility."

"I could be the financial backer. Gabe and the other brother—Josh, right?—will run the ranch."

This was absurd. Her father talked like the purchase was a done deal.

Reese's heart pounded. "You cannot do this, Dad! Think of the problems it will cause."

Gabe would be furious. And he might think she was encouraging her father, though she'd assured him she had no personal agenda.

Her father leveled a finger at her. "You don't get to tell me what to do, young lady."

She stood, her legs now strong. "You're

right. But I can tell Gabe about this, and I will. Right now."

Storm clouds gathered on her father's face, worrying her. She hadn't seen him this angry in a long time.

"Why would you go against me?" he demanded.

"Dad, I have a responsibility as trustee to oversee the finances of Dos Estrellas to the best of my ability."

"You also have an obligation to me."

"If owning a share of Dos Estrellas was in your best interest or good for your health, I'd support you a hundred percent. Neither one is the case. And I know for a fact Cole is after whatever money he can get his hands on. He has no loyalty to his brothers, Josh included."

She'd assumed, when he agreed to stay, he'd at least stick by Josh. Obviously not.

What a mess. She had to do something.

"He's making the decision that's best for him," her father said. "Nothing wrong with that."

"This isn't like you, Dad. It would be one thing for you to buy Dos Estrellas outright. Heaven knows you offered enough times. But to wrangle your way in the back door by taking advantage of a family dispute—"

"Now, wait a minute."

"I won't. In fact, I'm leaving now."

"Where are you going?"

To the only place that made any sense. "Our neighbors."

"Reese."

The pleading in her father's voice tore at her, and all at once she understood. He didn't want to own a one-third share of the Dos Estrellas, bought from a disgruntled brother. He would have owned the ranch outright, had the opportunity ever presented itself.

Her father was flexing what was left of his muscles in order to feel like his old self. She decided to cut him some slack.

"I have to tell Gabe. He has a right to know."

Her father stared at her, unwaveringly, for several seconds. Then he looked away. "Do what you must."

His obvious pain made her question her actions. She took his hand in hers, holding it to her chest, just above her heart.

"I love you, Dad."

He nodded.

"We're going to get through this."

He laughed without mirth. "Haven't you been listening to my doctors?"

"Parkinson's isn't fatal."

"Might as well be."

Tears pricked her eyes "New advances are being made every day."

"You talk like that support group leader."

Her father had attended exactly one meeting, declaring afterward that all those people moping and whining weren't for him. He'd go it alone.

But he wasn't alone. He had her.

"We have to keep hoping, Dad. *I* have to keep hoping. If not, I'll fall apart."

"You're a good daughter, Reese. I'm a blessed man."

He hadn't called himself blessed since being told his initial prognosis.

She kissed the back of his hand. "See you tonight when I get home. Call if you need anything."

"You fuss over me too much." His objection was delivered with affection.

Wasting no time, not even to eat, Reese returned to her car and drove to Dos Estrellas. On the drive, she called Gabe. He answered on the second ring.

"Hi, there."

Minor static in the background didn't distort the fondness in his voice—which would change the moment she told him her news.

"Are you free?" she asked.

"Now?"

"If that's okay."

"Sure. I'm in the toolshed. Let me clean up, and I'll meet you at the house. Mom and Cara aren't home. They're making the rounds in town. Thanking some of our friends for their help these last few weeks by delivering homemade tamales. They won't be home until late tonight."

Was he dropping a hint that they'd have some privacy? Reese worried he might be recalling their kiss, and she didn't want to mislead him. "We can do this another time."

"No. Come on by."

She could tell him on the phone and avoid an awkward situation. No, she needed to tell him her news face-to-face.

"See you in a few minutes."

Standing at Gabe's front door, she smoothed her slacks before ringing the bell. Someone, she guessed Raquel, had gone overboard decorating the house exterior and courtyard with lights, ornaments and a giant inflatable snow globe with Santa and Rudolph inside. An evergreen wreath hung from the door with a puffy red ribbon at its center. The half dozen organ-pipe cacti to the right of the door wore fake beards and Santa hats, the white tassels falling at jaunty angles.

Reese smiled. The next instant, guilt overwhelmed her. She'd been too busy with work and caring for her father to worry about decorating the house. Perhaps she should. It might cheer him. She'd loved the holidays as a kid, in part because her father always made a big production of them.

When no one answered the door, Reese knocked again. Gabe must be delayed. She rummaged in her purse for her cell phone, found it and groaned. She should have paid attention to the low battery warning. Now the phone was dead.

She began walking in the direction of the horse stable. If memory served, the toolshed was a dilapidated structure behind it. Hopefully, Gabe was still there.

She took a shortcut through the stables, the pointy heels of her boots sinking into the soft ground and hampering her progress. Were it a different day, she'd stop to pet the horses, especially Gabe's pretty mustang mare Bonita, who watched Reese with wide, chocolate eyes.

Reaching the end of the aisle, she turned the corner and came to an abrupt halt. It wasn't the toolshed with its repaired side-boards, new roof and fresh coat of paint that had given her pause. Rather, it was Gabe. He'd stripped off his jacket and rolled up his shirt sleeves. Bending over the open hood of the tractor, with his right arm buried in the engine up to his shoulder, he grimaced as if in pain.

Was he hurt? Caught his hand in some metal mechanism?

Reese quickened her steps. "Gabe, are you all right?"

"Hey." He opened his eyes, but didn't extract his arm. "Sorry. Thought I'd be finished by now."

"What happened? Can I help?"

"Tractor died in the middle of feeding this morning. It's the carburetor. I have this one last bolt to screw on."

"Oh. Okay." Feeling silly at panicking for no reason, she brushed self-consciously at her hair.

"Almost there." Groaning, he wiggled his arm. The bolt was obviously difficult to reach.

She waited, then swallowed. Gabe looked good. Heck, he always did. But today, his strong, athletic build was visible beneath his snug-fitting plaid shirt. The collar was open at his throat, revealing the muscles of his neck, which stood out as he strained to reattach the bolt.

Business, she reminded herself. She was here on business. Unpleasant business at that.

"No hurry," she said and turned her attention to the pasture. It was empty, except for two remaining towers of hay; the other three had been distributed to the cattle—and the cattle moved to yet another section. Sound management, in her opinion. Reserve the hay if possible.

"Could you hand me that towel?"

"Sure." She grabbed a crumpled hand towel lying on the tractor fender.

Gabe had withdrawn his arm from the engine while her back was to him. She was greeted by his broad chest and bare throat, three inches from her face.

Reese gasped and involuntarily stepped back. Her heel caught on a rock, and her ankle threatened to turn. She flailed, arms wind-milling.

He grabbed her by the shoulders and steadied her. "Whoa there."

His words were teasing. His tone, seductive. Reese responded by turning soft inside. When he dipped his head as if to kiss her, she came to her senses and held up a hand. "Wait. I have something to tell you. Something you won't like."

"What is it?" He didn't move, didn't release her and looked at her with such concern, such caring, she momentarily lost her train of thought.

"Your brother Cole," she finally managed to sputter. "He met with my father. Not an hour ago. And offered to sell him his share of Dos Estrellas."

"That son of a bitch."

Reese wasn't sure who Gabe was referring to, his brother or her father.

He released her, his arms falling away, his stare now cold as steel. "Was this your idea?"

"Gabe, how can you say that?" They'd kissed during the carriage ride. Talked intimately. "I wouldn't betray you. Neither would I jeopardize my job."

He stormed off.

She chased after him. "Where are you going?"

"To pay a call on your father."

"Gabe."

His pickup was parked near the barn, and he was on a collision course with it. "Butt out,

Reese. If this really wasn't your idea, then it doesn't concern you."

"There are things you don't know. About my father."

"I don't care." He yanked open the truck's driver's side door.

Reese couldn't let him get away. Couldn't let him storm her house and confront her father. Cutting in front of the truck, she hurried to the passenger side door.

"What are you doing?" Gabe growled when she climbed inside.

She prayed she was preventing a disaster. "If you're going to talk to my father, it'll be with me there."

Everything at the Small Change was twice as big as Dos Estrellas. The length of the driveway and the square arch adorning the entrance. The size of the main barn and livestock pens. The amount of grassland and grazing cattle. The height of the spouting water in the courtyard fountain. The damn wrought iron knocker on the front door.

Reese hadn't suggested that Gabe park around back, so he'd pulled his truck up parallel to the brick walkway leading to the front door. She'd come along, right beside him. So much for his plan of bursting in on her father unannounced.

They'd spoken once during the drive when she asked to use his phone, claiming hers was dead. He'd refused. Mean, yes, but he'd wanted whatever small advantage he could get.

Theo McGraw must have heard Gabe's truck screech to a gravel-spitting stop for he threw the door open just as Gabe crossed the threshold.

Taking in the two of them, he grinned affably. "Why am I not surprised?"

"Dad, Gabe wants to—"

Gabe cut her off. "I hope to hell you told Cole no."

He'd been in such an all-fire hurry to confront Theo, he'd forgotten to ask Reese how her father had responded to Cole's offer.

"Come in." Theo stepped back.

Gabe hesitated, afraid that accepting his enemy's invitation might show weakness. Ultimately, good manners prevailed, and he let Reese enter first. She'd hardly stepped across the threshold when he pushed inside.

Confronted by the beautifully appointed living room, with its cowhide-upholstered sofa, hand-carved bookcases and framed original oil paintings depicting cattle drives and local wildlife, Gabe stopped. He'd been to the Small Change before. A few times. Never inside the main house, though.

Were he calling on anyone else, he'd have commented on what a nice place they had.

"Can I offer you a drink?" Theo said. "Reese made some iced tea this morning."

"No, thank you."

"Sweetheart." He turned to Reese. "Can you give us a minute alone?"

"I don't think that's a good idea."

"I'm pretty sure our guest will conduct himself civilly." He raised a bushy brow at Gabe. "And I promise not to hit him unless he throws the first punch."

Reese sighed. "I'll be in the kitchen."

"No need to check on us unless I call for you."

She left the room reluctantly. Gabe wouldn't put it past her to hover nearby and eavesdrop.

"Now that she's gone." Theo McGraw rubbed his palms together. "Maybe I can interest you in a drink. Your father liked whiskey."

"Did he come here much?" Gabe was suddenly curious. "He never said."

"On occasion."

"What did Cole have to drink when he was here?"

Theo laughed and slapped his thigh.

Not that Gabe was well acquainted with the man, but there was something different about him. He looked older. Frailer. And there was a slight shakiness in his voice. When he walked over to the dry bar, his gait was slow and deliberate, as if he was carefully placing each foot in front of the other.

Going behind the bar, Theo removed two crystal tumblers from the shelf and a fifth of whiskey from the cabinet. "Straight up?"

Gabe was about to refuse. Again, he reconsidered, not wanting to appear weak. "Only if you'll join me."

"With pleasure." Theo's grin grew wider. "My daughter is going to have a fit. I'm not supposed to drink."

"Then I'll pass." Gabe ambled to the bar.

"Not on your life. It's not every day the son of August Dempsey pays me a visit. That's reason to celebrate."

Cole had visited Theo earlier, yet he'd referred to Gabe as August Dempsey's son. Against his will, Gabe warmed to his host.

Theo poured, a bit sloppily. Whiskey splashed onto the bar counter. He passed

Gabe the first glass. When he was done pouring his own, he raised his glass in toast. "To
August."

A moment ago, Gabe had been ready to
throttle Theo. Now, they clinked glasses and
tossed back their shots of whiskey. Gabe's
burned going down. Not in a bad way.

"You didn't answer my question," he said
when he could speak again.

Theo coughed, wheezed and pounded his
chest. "No, I didn't offer Cole a drink."

Gabe almost smiled. Theo was no dummy,
and he could play with the best of them. "Did
you turn him down?"

"I said I'd think about it."

"Don't buy his share of Dos Estrellas."

Theo met his gaze head on. "Why shouldn't
I?"

Gabe wasn't about to admit his plans to buy
out his brothers, to Theo. "Because you're a
better man than to kick someone when they're
down. And, much as I hate to admit it, we're
down. Deep down in a financial hole."

"I've had my eye on your ranch for a lot of
years. Here's my opportunity."

"You'd be buying into a lot of debt."

"True." He sipped at the remainder of his
whiskey rather than gulping it, a look of

contentment on his face. "This hits the spot. Reese complains if I drink, says it's bad for my...health."

"She doesn't want you to buy Cole's share."

Theo raised an eyebrow. "She tell you that?"

Gabe shook his head. "She came over to warn me about Cole. It's almost the same thing."

"Always had a moral compass, that one. She could have blamed me for her mother leaving. I wasn't the best husband." His expression turned tender. "She didn't. Stayed by me."

"Mr. McGraw."

"Call me Theo."

Gabe exhaled slowly. He wasn't in the mood to indulge the other man's stroll down memory lane. "Okay, Theo. I can't stop Cole from selling you his share, and I can't stop you from buying it. But I'm asking you to give me six months."

"What happens then?"

"*I'm* going to buy Cole's share. Hopefully, Josh's, too."

"Why would I wait?"

Gabe didn't have the chance to answer.

"How's it going?" Reese asked as she entered the living room, clearly defying her father's wishes. She glanced first at her father, then Gabe.

Theo laughed and slapped his thigh again. "The girl can't take orders. You should remember that."

Gabe wondered if Theo knew about him and Reese. No, impossible.

"As you can see, dear daughter," Theo continued, "we're both still in one piece. No punches thrown."

Gabe swore under his breath. He hadn't had a chance to finish his conversation with Theo, and he wouldn't in front of Reese. "I'd better go."

"Nonsense," Theo said. "You're my guest. Stay."

"Are you drinking whiskey?" Reese marched over to him, then frowned at Gabe. "Was this your idea?"

"Don't blame him," said Theo. "I'm the one who broke out the bottle."

"Dad!" She squeezed her eyes shut.

Gabe didn't need to witness the McGraw family dynamics. He had plenty of his own. "If you'll excuse me."

He started for the door and got no more than three feet before Theo lost his balance, banged into the bar and then hit the floor with an agonizing cry.

"Dad!"

Gabe rushed to Theo and knelt beside him. "Are you hurt?"

"I'm fine," he grumbled. "Damned rug."

It wasn't the rug. The older man's legs had simply gone out from under him.

By now, Reese was also kneeling beside her father. "Did you hit your head?"

"My elbow." He tried pushing up, only to collapse in either exhaustion or pain.

"Let me." Gabe stood and, getting a firm grip on Theo's uninjured arm, lifted him to a sitting position.

Theo sat and held his head as if the room was spinning. "Give me a minute."

Gabe gave him three before assisting him to his feet. Next, he carefully walked Theo to the nearest chair and sat him down.

"I'll get you some water," Reese said.

"I'm not thirsty."

"You shouldn't have been drinking."

"Please quit your nagging." Rather than harsh, Theo's request was imploring.

Gabe could see Reese struggled to keep quiet. "Should we call 9-1-1?" he asked.

"Maybe." She chewed her bottom lip.

"Hell, no!"

"If you can protest like that," Gabe gripped Theo's shoulder, "then you must be feeling better."

Neither Reese nor her father acknowledged his joke. Their worried faces indicated more going on. What was it Reese had told Gabe back at Dos Estrellas before he'd made a mad dash for his truck?

There are things you don't know. About my father.

Whereas Gabe had been anxious to leave a short time ago, he was now hesitant.

"I'm going to call your doctor," Reese said.

"And have him charge me another co-pay." Theo shook his head. "Not on your life."

"Let me see your elbow." She reached for him.

He, in turn, yanked his injured arm out of her reach. "Leave me alone, dagnabbit."

Various versions of this same exchange continued for several more minutes. Gabe saw that Theo was growing stronger. When he felt relatively certain his host was in no immediate danger, he said, "I'm going to let you two hammer this out alone."

"Wait." Theo grabbed Gabe's wrist. His

grip was surprisingly strong. "I'll give you that six months."

Gabe nodded. "I appreciate it."

"On one condition. You tell no one what happened."

He didn't need to elaborate. Gabe understood. For whatever reason, Theo wanted his fall to remain a secret.

"Agreed."

"Reese." Theo hitched his chin at the door. "Would you be so kind as to see our guest out?"

"My car," she exclaimed, suddenly remembering. "It's at Gabe's house."

"I'll drive it here later. Have someone follow me."

"She needs to get back to work," Theo said.

"No, I don't. I called in while you two were talking and told Walt I was taking the afternoon off."

"Good." Theo smiled for the first time since his fall. "Then you can go back with Gabe and fetch your car."

"I'm not leaving you alone." She crossed her arms.

"I told you, I'm perfectly fine."

"You're not." Tears filled her voice.

"Call Enrico." Theo's shoulders slumped

in defeat. "It's about time for his afternoon report."

Reese looked at Gabe. "Give me a minute."

Gabe sat on one of the two bar stools. "Take your time."

"She's become quite the mother hen," Theo said when Reese left the room.

"She loves you."

"I'm a lucky man."

"You are."

"The man who wins her heart will be lucky, too."

Gabe nodded, not sure how to reply.

Reese wasn't gone long. They waited another few minutes for Enrico to arrive. Gabe doubted his appearance was solely to report the day's activity to Theo, though the two of them discussed an upcoming cold front. Gabe noticed a look pass between Reese and the burly ranch foreman. If he interpreted it correctly, she was saying, "Call me later."

This arrangement, Theo falling and Enrico caring for him under the guise of ranch business, didn't appear to be anything new. Gabe remembered Reese getting a call when her father fell off the porch. And there had been that tremor when he'd poured the shots of whiskey. The man was ill.

Outside, Gabe opened his truck door for Reese, chagrined at his earlier behavior. When she asked if she could use his phone charger, he plugged it in for her.

At Dos Estrellas, he parked next to her car in the driveway. He knew he should let her leave, but he couldn't. Opening her car door, he took her hand and prevented her from climbing in behind the steering wheel.

"What's wrong with your father?"

Tears welled in her eyes.

"You came and told me about Cole. You didn't have to. I realize now I can trust you. You can trust me, too. I've proven myself."

His reminder of their prom night broke down her defenses, and she sobbed softly. "He has Parkinson's."

Gabe put an arm around her and pulled her to him. "Oh, honey, I'm sorry." He knew better than many what it was like to deal with a severely ill parent. "Come inside. We'll talk."

She shook her head.

"Call Enrico. Tell him to make up an excuse to stay with your dad. You need to vent before you have a breakdown."

Truthfully, he expected her to refuse. She didn't. Arm in arm, they walked inside the house.

Chapter 10

"Coffee?"

For a second, Reese almost answered Gabe's question with *I'd prefer a whiskey,* but instead bit her tongue. Much as she might like to follow her father's example and indulge in a dose of liquid courage, she was better off with caffeine. Whiskey might break down her last hold on her emotions, and she'd wind up a weeping mess. Once, in Gabe's company, was enough.

"Sure. Thanks."

A gourmet single-serving coffee maker sat on the kitchen counter. While Gabe prepared two cups with practiced ease, Reese threw her coat over the back of the nearest chair and sat at the table. The house was quiet, reminding her that his mother and Cara were gone until late this evening. His brothers, staying in the guest suite, used a separate entrance and, according to Gabe, came into the main house strictly for meals. She and Gabe were completely alone.

Good, when it came to taking him up on his offer for a heartfelt talk. Bad, when it came to their wildly exciting, but inappropriate, attraction. With the way she was feeling right now, getting cozy with Gabe was the last thing on her mind.

Well, maybe not the *last* thing. He did have a way of consuming her every thought by simply entering the room. And there was something deliciously thrilling about them being alone. Especially during Thanksgiving dinner when Raquel had sent them to the garage on the pretense of fetching the platter, they hadn't been truly isolated.

"Does anyone besides me know about your dad's Parkinson's?" Gabe set a steaming mug in front of her, then, removing his cowboy hat and setting it on the counter, occupied the adjacent chair. He cradled his own mug of coffee between his hands. "Besides you and Enrico."

"Enrico doesn't know. Not exactly. I'm convinced he suspects Dad's ill, but he's very loyal and won't say a word."

She stared at her mug. The coffee was black.

"Is something wrong?" Gabe asked.

"I hate to be a bother."

"You?" he teased.

A different day, a different moment when she wasn't hurting, she'd laugh. "Do you have any creamer?"

He produced three varieties from the refrigerator. "Cara's doing."

Reese selected the mocha-flavored creamer. "I got addicted to this stuff in high school."

"You used to go to the Java Stop after school. I'd see you there."

She and her group of friends had thought they were cool, frequenting the popular hangout and ordering specialty overpriced coffee drinks. How silly. "You noticed me?"

His tone became soft and low. "I noticed a lot of things about you."

Noticed *and* remembered. She was touched, flattered and more enamored than ever. "I wish we'd been friends back then."

"I wished we'd dated."

"As I recall, you didn't like me much."

"You never gave me a chance."

She didn't quite believe him. Their fathers had greatly influenced them when they were younger and not much had changed. Even now Reese could feel her father yanking the invisible strings attached to her.

"I appreciate you respecting Dad's request to not tell anyone about his Parkinson's."

"Like I said, you can trust me."

"You've kept my secret for twelve years. If I haven't said so before, I appreciate it."

He shrugged.

"You're an honorable man, Gabe. It's a quality not everyone has."

"Telling people about your father won't serve any purpose."

"He's afraid it would discredit him. If you wanted, you could use that to your advantage. Buyers might hesitate to deal with someone who's sick and throw business your way."

"Your father has some physical limitations. I can assure you, though, he's still sharp as a tack."

"Oh, yes. I can attest to that." The hot coffee felt good going down her throat. Holding back her tears this past hour had left it raw. "I just wish he'd let me hire a part-time caregiver. I can't provide everything he needs and half of what I can, he won't let me. Too proud."

She'd offered to help him bathe, shave, dress and a dozen other personal tasks. His response had been to snap at her. Yesterday, he'd sliced his finger with a pocketknife while trying to clean his fingernails, then refused to let her clean and bandage the small wound. He'd be lucky if he didn't get an infection.

"It's hard on me," she said, her voice cracking. "The extra work, the emotional stress, seeing him hurt himself. This wasn't his first fall."

"Have you told him how hard it is on you?"

"I don't want to get into an argument."

"He needs to know he's making your life difficult."

"Not difficult. I love my father."

"We went through the same thing with my dad. He ran Mom ragged. It got to a point where *her* health was in jeopardy."

Reese swiped at her eyes. She could see the same happening to her.

"I remember the name of the nursing service we used. They were good. We hired a male nurse. Dad was more comfortable with him than a woman."

Her father would be, too. "Maybe. Let me think about it."

"You'll be no good to your father if you're worn out."

"I'm more worried about my job. I'm finding it harder and harder to concentrate. I don't want to start making mistakes."

Almost at once, she regretted her words. Would Gabe jump to the conclusion she wasn't doing her best as trustee?

"You're too smart for that," he said.

His assurances didn't ease her concerns. But when he folded her hand in his and squeezed her fingers, a calmness spread slowly through her, and she welcomed it.

"I like you, Gabe." Closing her eyes, she grimaced. "I shouldn't have said that."

"I'm glad you did. I like you, too."

"A lot." Oh, God, this was getting worse by the second.

His grip on her hand tightened. "I know."

"Oh? You do?"

"You kissed me, Reese. I may be an insensitive lug, but I can tell when a woman's into me."

"Into you?" She almost pulled her hand

away, but didn't. "You sound pretty confident."

"What I am is glad. I'd hate to think I'm the only one losing my heart here."

Her pulse quickened. "Gabe, we can't let this go any further. It's okay to flirt a bit and maybe kiss, but no more and not again."

"Hmm." He grinned, and her pulse literally skipped a beat. "And here I was thinking of taking things further."

"You're terrible. That wasn't funny."

"I'm not joking."

He wasn't. She could tell by the look in his eyes, which roved her face as if trying to memorize every nuance. This intense scrutiny was incredibly more flattering and harder to resist.

"What are we going to do about it?" he asked.

She tensed. Was he serious? "Nothing."

"You're entitled to be happy."

"Not at the expense of my job."

"Is there a bank policy against dating customers?"

"Not exactly. Any romantic relationships must be disclosed." Reese imagined herself having that conversation with Walt and cringed. No way. "My boss would think I've lost my mind."

"You're right." Gabe let go of her hand. "It's a bad idea."

She hadn't expected him to acquiesce so quickly and thought of telling him she'd reconsidered. Maybe then he'd hold her hand again and stare into her eyes.

"I should probably get go—"

He cut her off. "You don't have to. Whatever it is you were going to say."

His voice was rich with promise and his smile contained a hint of mischief. The combination was too appealing for her own good.

"Yes, I do." Yes, she *should*.

"Keep looking at me the way you are and I won't be responsible for my actions."

She knew he wanted her. Like he'd said, they'd kissed. He wasn't the only one who could gauge a person's feelings. Neither was he the only one staring with an unmistakable hunger in their eyes.

"You could walk me to my car," she suggested.

"I'm going to do more than that." He pushed back from the table and stood. Taking her hand, he helped her to her feet and, before she could stop him, into his arms.

"Gabe. Didn't we agree—"

"To heed our better judgment and not make costly mistakes. Kissing you is no mistake."

"We're asking for trouble."

"I kind of like getting into trouble with you."

She might have said more but she couldn't. Her mouth was otherwise occupied. She let him take the lead, fusing her lips to his, then parting them. He wasted no time, tasting and teasing and satisfying her.

No, there was no satisfying. Regardless of what she'd said earlier, she craved more. While his hands roamed her back, she linked her arms around his neck and sifted her fingers through his hair. At his low moan of pleasure, she grew bolder and arched into him, her breasts making exhilarating contact with the hard planes of his chest.

He tensed and withdrew, gazing at her like she was everything in the world to him. "You're incredible."

"I think it takes two to achieve incredible."

"How did we not figure this out before?"

She shook her head, not sure what to say. Had she gone after the wrong man, Blake, because the right man, Gabe, was someone her father didn't approve of?

His hands settled on the curves of her hips and pulled her close. He moaned again. Reese didn't consider herself to be particularly sexy, but turning him on, obviously exciting him, gave her a heady sensation she could get used to.

Saying no to the many wonderful, exciting possibilities that could be hers if she'd simply give in would be harder than she'd imagined. "Gabe. Please—"

The floor shifted beneath her. She uttered a cry before realizing Gabe had picked her up. Turning in a half circle, he deposited her on the table. Not giving her a chance to catch her breath, he kneed her legs apart and positioned himself between them.

Speaking wasn't possible. At first, because he'd left her speechless. Then because he was kissing her again, with an intensity and passion that drove all but the last shred of good judgment from her mind.

He leaned into her. For an insane second, she thought he might be trying to lay her back on the table. The next instant, her relieved mind registered he was simply closing the distance between their bodies to nothing but a few molecules of thin air.

Heaven help her, she abandoned control

and let him kiss her. His tongue swept into her mouth, evoking greater thrills with each stroke. His hands pressed into the small of her back and, when she moved her hips encouragingly, dipped into the waistband of her slacks. He must have realized she wore the briefest of panties for he let out a low, desperate sound that sent a shiver of pleasure coursing through her.

"I want you, Reese."

All at once, he really was laying her back onto the table. She immediately grasped that last shred of good judgment and ended their kiss.

"No. We can't."

He pulled back and, breathing deeply, lifted her off the table and onto her feet. "We could go to my room."

They could. His mother and Cara were gone for hours.

They *couldn't*! No matter how Reese felt about Gabe, and she was starting to care more than she'd have ever believed possible, she refused to endanger her job. They'd already crossed the line. Several times. To plunge headlong into dangerous territory was career suicide.

Placing her palm on the front of his shirt,

she backed away. "I won't do something we'll both regret."

He hesitated a moment. Reese thought he might continue attempting to sway her. He didn't, surprising her once again.

"I understand." He tried a smile, which fell short. "I apologize for getting carried away."

"My fault, too."

"You have to admit." His smile widened. "It was a great kiss."

The best ever. He'd literally and figuratively swept her off her feet. "One for the record books."

He grabbed her jacket from the back of the chair and held it out for her. "I'll walk you to your car."

She slipped her right arm into the sleeve, then her left one and adjusted the jacket before buttoning it. Her exit did seem hasty, though under the circumstances, probably wise. Her defenses were at an all-time low.

At her car, he bent and gave her a sweet, yet lingering kiss that was completely intoxicating.

"Wait for me, Reese," he said and nuzzled her ear. "I've got a plan."

"For what?" He could be very distracting.

"Give me six months. I'm going to buy out my brothers."

She couldn't imagine how, as she'd turned down his one request to draw on the line of credit. Gabe was quite determined, though. Perhaps more now than before.

Rather than mention the many obstacles he faced, she hugged him to her.

"I'll help any way I can."

"I won't jeopardize your job."

Reese believed him. He hadn't let her down in the past.

She couldn't be with Gabe, not the way she longed to be, body and soul and heart. For now, she'd be content to wait. After today, and what had transpired between them, she believed they had what it took for a lasting relationship. That was certainly worth waiting a measly six months.

"Will your children be here for Christmas?" Gabe's mother asked Josh. "It would be so nice to have little ones in the house again."

Cara hadn't joined them for breakfast, otherwise his mother wouldn't have mentioned children and Christmas for fear of upsetting her.

"I'm afraid not," Josh said. "This will be

their last time with their mother for a while. I agreed to let her have them for the holidays."

Gabe didn't know the whole story, but Josh had said something about his ex-wife going into rehab—her third go-round—for a drug addiction problem, which was one of the reasons he'd gained full custody of their kids.

"I won't be getting them until mid-January." Josh poured himself a glass of orange juice, then passed the pitcher to Cole.

Breakfast with his brothers had become something of a ritual for Gabe, thanks to his mother and her insistence. Conversation was mostly between her and Josh. Gabe and Cole preferred the roles of spectators.

He had yet to tell Cole he knew about his trip to see Theo McGraw. Gabe also hadn't told anyone about Theo's Parkinson's. Yesterday, Reese had called and asked him the name of the home nursing service they'd used when his father was ill. Perhaps she was making progress with Theo.

He hoped so. He was anxious for her to become a part of his life. But before that could happen, she needed to delegate some of her responsibilities for her father's care to a reliable nurse. Also, be done with her duties as trustee of Gabe's father's estate, which would occur when he bought out his brothers' shares.

"Oh, Josh." His mother clucked sympathetically as she crossed from the stove to the kitchen table, delivering a bowl heaped with scrambled eggs. "That is too bad for you, but good for the children's mother. It's important she have the support of her family during such a difficult time."

"Yeah. You're right." He didn't sound convinced.

Gabe's mother smiled delightedly. "I can't wait to meet them. A girl and a boy. The perfect family."

He didn't point out that if Josh was divorced and his ex-wife about to enter rehab for the third time, they were hardly the perfect family.

"I appreciate all you've done for us." Josh helped her find a place for the bowl, then sent his brother a sharp look.

"Yes. Thanks, Raquel," Cole said.

They'd been behaving better since the scene during Thanksgiving dinner. Perhaps due to Gabe and his suggestion they work together. He liked to think so, anyway.

"*De nada.*" His mother beamed as she took her seat.

What would she do if she learned that, a mere few days ago, Reese had been sitting on the table, right where his mother's arm rested, and Gabe had been kissing her like a crazy man, hoping to steal her off to his bedroom?

She'd box his ears, like she'd done that time when he was seven and, on a dare, had stolen a pack of gum from the market. She'd also probably insist he make an honest woman out of Reese, though they hadn't let things go far enough to warrant a hasty wedding.

Funny, the idea of a future with Reese didn't scare Gabe like it had with his former girlfriends. Later, he'd give the notion some thoughtful consideration.

Or not. Frankly, it didn't matter. Gabe wasn't considering anything more serious than dating Reese. For now.

"Gabe, will you drive me to the lot by the market today for a Christmas tree?"

Gabe returned his attention to his mother. She'd been asking for this favor all week, and he couldn't put her off any longer.

"Yes, but not until after supper. We're meeting with the vet to decide on which cows to breed. If you can wait, I'm all yours."

Josh and Cole would also be at the meeting in order to learn, though Violet was technically in charge. Before the cancer had struck his father, Dos Estrellas owned several bulls, using them for breeding. The bulls, proven producers with outstanding lines, were the first livestock to be sold. As a result, this year they would artificially inseminate the cows.

The three brothers and Violet had much work ahead of them. To ensure the best results and produce a bumper number of calves at the least cost, the artificial insemination must be done as precisely as possible.

"I spoke to Tio Lorenzo yesterday," Gabe's mother said, referring to her favorite brother. "He's coming for Christmas."

"That's great, Mom."

His mother was very close to her brothers, Lorenzo in particular. The upcoming visit had made her very happy. Just as his grandparents' refusal to visit made her sad.

"I'm looking forward to meeting him," Josh said.

He, at least, was being a good houseguest. Cole continued to eat in disgruntled silence.

What, Gabe wondered, had made his brother unhappy? Was being here, living in the home of the father he'd hated, the sole reason or was it something else? Why, Gabe wondered, did he care? He shouldn't waste his mental energy. Cole didn't spend one second thinking about him.

But Gabe did find himself thinking and caring. Reese was responsible for the change in him. Because of her, and their unexpected feelings, he had begun to look at his brothers differently.

"It's going to be a nice Christmas this year." His mother smiled at each of them.

Much better than the previous two. Though they would all miss his father terribly, and remember the loss of Cara's son, he, like his mother, had something positive to look forward to.

When they were done eating, Josh offered to help with the dishes, a chore Cara usually did. Not to be outdone, Gabe cleared the table. He was carting the last of the dirty plates to the counter when his cell phone rang.

He didn't recognize the number, but the voice that greeted him was familiar. Buck Sadoski, the cattle broker he'd spoken with several weeks earlier, was in high spirits.

"Hey, partner, how are you this glorious morning?" His booming voice resounded in Gabe's ear.

"Good. And yourself?" He hadn't expected to hear from Buck this soon; the cattle broker hadn't taken it well when Gabe turned down his previous generous offer.

"Fine and dandy."

"What can I do for you?" Gabe excused himself to his father's office with a wave to his mother. He didn't want his family to over-hear his conversation.

"Partner, it's what I can do for you. I have four hundred of the best-looking steer calves you've seen in all your born days en route to Phoenix from Texas right this minute. They'll be hitting the borders of our fair city by to-morrow morning. I'm looking for a buyer, and the first person I thought of was you."

Normally, Gabe would be interested only in cows or heifers, seeing as breeding season was well upon them. And, after the last fi-asco when Reese refused to advance him the purchase money, he was reluctant to jump in with both feet.

"Not sure I'm in the market for steer."

Buck laughed, low and grumbly. "Wait until I tell you the price."

He did, and Gabe's interest flared.

"You hold on to these little fellows until this spring, fatten 'em up, and you can sell them for a tidy profit."

That, he could.

"Beef prices are going to continue to soar," Buck added. "Count on it."

Gabe quickly ran the numbers in his head. If beef prices rose even half of what those in the business were predicting, they could stand to make 30 percent on their investment.

They, or him? What if he were to buy the calves on his own? Without his brothers?

Naw, he couldn't pull it off. Not without drawing on the line of credit, and Reese had made it clear that was impossible without his brothers' knowledge and consent. There was also the matter of supplemental feed. With more head, they would have to purchase additional hay, and maybe not at the good price Banner Hay Sales had given them last time.

To make a purchase of this size, including the cattle and the hay, they'd quite possibly use what was left of the line of credit after paying for inseminating the cows.

Risky, yes, but not much of a risk. Young steers could be counted on to grow up.

"You don't take these pretty babies," Buck said, "and someone else will."

In a heartbeat. The man wasn't exaggerating. It was a good deal. If Gabe were to approach his brothers, he'd have to sell them on the idea. He had no idea how they'd react.

"Have the calves been vet checked?"

Buck chuckled. "I'm staring at the paperwork right here in front of me."

"Give me until the end of the day," Gabe said.

"Sorry." The cattle broker didn't sound sorry. "I've got to have these babies sold before the trucks arrive tomorrow. If you don't want them, I know ten other ranchers who do."

Buck wasn't exaggerating about that, either.

"Can you give me two hours?"

"Okay. But if I don't hear from you by nine o'clock, I'm gonna start making calls."

Gabe thanked him and hung up, then returned to the kitchen. Josh and his mother were finishing up with the dishes.

"Where's Cole?" he asked, then did a double take.

Josh wore a dish towel as an apron and was chatting amiably with his mother. They made a curious and unsettling picture. At Gabe's question, Josh glanced over his shoulder. "In the barn. He's driving out with Violet this morning."

That was right. They were distributing the last of the hay.

Gabe punched Cole's number into his phone.

"What's up?" Josh asked, his brows forming a deep V as he walked over to where Gabe stood.

"We have a lead on four hundred steer at a smokin' price."

"Can we afford them?"

"I don't think we can afford not to buy them. Hey, Cole," he said when his younger brother picked up. "Get yourself back to the house. We have an emergency meeting."

Gabe's father had conducted all his business in his office. Gabe broke with tradition. While his mother busied herself elsewhere in the house, he, Josh and Cole hammered out the details at the kitchen table.

It wasn't easy. They didn't always agree. Neither was it hard. Both Josh and Cole deferred to Gabe as the more experienced one among them.

At a quarter till nine, Gabe called Buck and told him that they would buy the steer. Their next call was to Reese. Gabe didn't ask for the money. Instead, he inquired when she'd be free to see them. He kept the conversation strictly business, never once slipping into the familiarity they'd shared often these past weeks.

"We have something to discuss with you."

"We?" Reese sounded busy.

"Me and my brothers."

"All right."

She agreed to see them after lunch. Gabe spent the time with Violet and his brothers, readying the pastures in the upper sections. He envisioned the young steers roaming Dos Estrellas pastures, growing fat and sleek, then using his share of the profits when the steer were sold to realize all his dreams.

It might not be a sure thing, but it wasn't impossible, either. Gabe could do it if he worked hard and stayed the course.

Chapter 11

Two wranglers lifted the ramp on the last trailer truck and closed it. The safety bar fell into place with a resounding clang.

The wrangler on the left, a wizened old-timer, secured the latch and called to his buddy, "We're done. Load up."

The pair jogged to the cab of the truck, one on each side of the long metal trailer, and clamored inside. They waved as they pulled out, joining the rest of the caravan waiting on the main road.

"Wow." Reese showered Gabe with a brilliant smile. "Been a while since I've seen this many young steer."

"I could say the same."

His gaze traveled the length of the herd, which stretched out nearly a quarter mile as the steer strolled leisurely across the pasture, enjoying their freedom as they familiarized themselves with their new home. More hay would be delivered tomorrow. Gabe hoped this would be their last purchase for a while.

Finally, the skies were an ominous gray and heavy with cloud cover. Rain was predicted to fall by evening. It was the Christmas present Gabe had wanted most, and, while early by a couple of weeks, it appeared he was going to get his wish.

"I've *never* see this many steer," Josh added, a trace of awe in his voice. "Not all in one place."

The three of them sat astride their horses, Gabe on Bonita, Reese on her father's horse General, who was fully recovered from his fall in the sinkhole, and Josh on one of Cole's fancy roping horses he'd brought from California.

Gabe would rather he and Reese be alone. He'd like to express his excitement and appreciation in a way involving their mouths making intimate contact. Instead, he'd had to thank her the polite and proper way, by shaking her hand.

With the three brothers in agreement, Reese had reluctantly, but willingly, authorized the draw on the line of credit. There wasn't much remaining after paying the cattle broker and Banner Hay Sales. Barely enough to cover the cost of artificially inseminating the cows.

Reese worried that, should an emergency arise, Dos Estrellas would be at risk without the benefit of a reserve. However, purchasing the steer, inseminating the cows, growing the herd, it was all part of Gabe's father's plan. She'd been ultimately swayed by both the excellent price of the steer and the brothers' unanimous consent.

"How'd you convince them?" she'd asked at the bank after their meeting.

Gabe had leaned close and dipped his head. "I can be persuasive."

She'd gasped in shock and quickly shooed him out her office door. But when he'd asked her if she wanted to join them for the delivery of the steer, she'd heartily agreed, which had gladdened Gabe. He'd been missing her something terrible.

"I'm going to ride up the hill a bit," he said.

"Inspect that fence we repaired. Make sure it holds."

They didn't need any of the steers to bust through the fence and onto Small Change land.

"I'll go with you." Reese turned General in Gabe's direction.

He expected Josh to tag along and was pleased when his brother begged off with, "I'm going to ride back to the ranch and give Violet a hand."

Finally, thought Gabe, some time alone with Reese.

Reese glanced back at his brother more than once as she and Gabe ascended the sloping hill, her lovely brow knitted in concentration. "Do you think he's interested in her?"

"Josh and Violet?" Gabe's first reaction was to laugh. His second was to frown. "I don't know. I don't think so."

"They've been working together a lot recently."

"I suppose." Gabe studied the sky. He could smell rain in the air, and it raised his spirits almost as much as seeing all those young steer roaming the pastures.

"They're both single," Reese continued, the wind stealing her words and swallowing them.

"He hasn't said anything to me."

"Would he?" She shot Gabe a sideways look that implied he was being a bit dense.

He shrugged, not the least offended. "Doubtful."

"I think they'd make a cute couple."

"He hasn't asked about her." If Gabe was interested in a woman, he'd find out what he could. "Besides, Cole spends more time with her than Josh."

"Well," Reese scoffed, "nothing's going to happen between *them*."

Gabe tended to agree. Cole told anyone who cared to listen that his ambition remained the same. Leave Mustang Valley at the first opportunity.

"How's your dad?" he asked, changing the subject.

"About the same."

Seeing the light leave her eyes, Gabe was sorry he'd brought up the subject.

"No more falls, thank goodness," she said. "And he finally told Enrico about his Parkinson's, though I think what actually happened is Enrico confronted him. Dad won't say."

By unspoken agreement, they stopped their horses and watched the steer nibble at the sparse grass on their slow trek to the stock pond over the next rise. Tomorrow morning, after breakfast, Violet would supervise the delivery of the first load of hay. Josh would probably help her.

Could Reese be right? Was an attraction developing between Josh and Violet? If true, Gabe wasn't sure how he felt about that. He wanted his livestock manager's undivided loyalty.

"I think it was hard for Dad, telling Enrico." Reese pulled her knit scarf up around her ears to ward off the cold, tucking the tails inside her jacket.

Gabe instantly recalled nuzzling those ears during their heated kiss on the carriage ride. He'd nuzzled her neck during their kiss in the kitchen.

What would she say if he climbed down from his horse right now and—

"I hired a part-time nurse," Reese said, interrupting his thoughts. "It was a tough battle, getting Dad to agree."

"What changed his mind?"

"His doctor. They had a long heart-to-heart last week. Actually, I think what the doctor gave Dad was a severe talking-to, but that's not how Dad described it."

"You might want to consider getting medical power of attorney soon. We did with my dad. Saved us a lot of hassle in dealing with his doctors."

"I suppose I'll have to eventually." Reese sighed. "For now, I'm taking things slowly. Hiring the part-time nurse was a first step."

Because her mood had visibly changed at the mention of her father, Gabe dropped the subject. She could use a break from the stress at home, not have him add to it.

"Don't overwork yourself at Christmas," he said, remembering how his mother had run herself ragged. Her efforts to care for his father, play hostess to her visiting family and fill the house with as much cheer as possible had left her exhausted and miserable. "The holidays can be rough with a sick family member."

"My aunt Louise wanted to come for a visit. Dad told her no."

Reese sounded disappointed, and Gabe longed to comfort her. "You could visit her."

She shook her head. "I can't leave Dad."

"Why don't I invite you both for Christmas dinner at our house? Mom would love it."

Her lush mouth curved into a smile, reminding him of how much he wanted to kiss her. "We both know how that ended the first time."

"Strangely enough, I think it might go better than Thanksgiving."

"You three have made some amazing progress in getting along."

"Things are going to work out, Reese." He grinned.

"You sound confident."

"I am."

Her smile widened, some of its former brilliance returning.

He was captivated. "If you need any help with your dad, let me know."

"Thank you."

Impulsively, he reached across the small distance separating them and grabbed her hand, clutching it in his.

"We shouldn't," she warned, glancing around.

"No one's here to see us."

"I suppose not."

"I've missed you," Gabe said, feeling uncharacteristically vulnerable.

"Me, too." Her expression shone with sincerity. "Missed you."

Perhaps she wouldn't be opposed to that kiss after all. Gabe was wondering how to pull it off exactly when one of the young steer caught his eye.

It had wandered away from the herd, about one hundred feet away. Unusual behavior, as cattle were naturally wary of horses with riders, but not unheard of. It was the steer's stilted and awkward gait that set off silent alarms in Gabe's head. The steer walked stiffly as if its joints hurt.

"Look." He dropped Reese's hand in order to point.

"What am I looking at?"

"The steer separated from the rest. Something's not right with him."

Rather than ride over, Gabe dismounted. With any luck, he'd be able to get close to the steer on foot.

Fifty or so of the steer nearest them stared in comical, wide-eyed unison. They didn't bolt, which was a relief. Gabe was in a vulnerable position if they chose to run at him.

About twenty feet away from the steer, Gabe halted. He didn't like what he saw. Fluid dripped from the steer's nostrils and its nose gleamed a bright red color. Combine those symptoms with the steer's stilted movement and vacant stare, and Gabe had reason to worry.

He studied the other nearby steer for several minutes, which quickly lost interest in him and continued meandering down the hill. At first, all appeared to be in good health. Active, alert and munching grass. Then, Gabe saw it. Another steer with clear fluid dripping from its nostrils.

No point in panicking, he told himself as a jolt of fear shot through him. Returning to Bonita, he swung up into the saddle.

"I need to get back to the ranch. Fast."

"What is it?" Her voice rose with concern.

"A couple of the steer are sick. I'm going to call the vet. Have him get over here right away."

"Sick? The herd was vet checked. You got the papers."

He had. But, as anyone in the ranching business knew, cattle could appear perfectly healthy one day and drop dead the next. Some diseases progressed that quickly.

He urged Bonita into a lope. Reese rode beside him, down the hill and toward Dos Estrellas. There wasn't a moment to waste.

Two or three sick cattle wasn't unusual. Viruses were common and not necessarily cause for concern. If the steer had contracted something more serious, then Gabe—and his entire family—could be in serious trouble.

As much as Gabe had wanted to be alone with Reese earlier, he'd have liked nothing better than for her to disappear when the vet arrived to examine the sickly steer. But she had remained. Not as his potential romantic interest and not as his friend. She'd stayed as trustee of his father's estate, watching and, he was sure of it, forming opinions.

She'd been present when the vet had delivered the agonizing news. The steer, over thirty in all, and with that number potentially growing by the hour, were stricken with infectious bovine rhinotracheitis. Red nose, the local ranchers called it. There was no definitive medical test, but the vet was adamant. He'd seen enough cases.

"I don't understand," Reese said. "Weren't the steer vaccinated?"

They stood outside the main barn, having returned minutes ago from meticulously inspecting and subsequently treating the infected steer. In addition to Gabe, Reese and the vet—a small, wiry man with impressive strength and stamina—Violet was also present.

At least Josh and Cole wouldn't see Gabe's

humiliation. Cara had called asking for help at the mustang sanctuary, and he'd quickly dispatched his brothers.

"They were," Violet answered Reese's question. "I read the paperwork myself."

Four people in total had, including Reese, before the money changed hands. She knew that. Gabe wasn't sure why she'd asked. Unless it was to drive home the point that he alone was responsible as the person whose idea it was to buy the steer.

"Vaccinations are no guarantee a herd won't become infected," the vet said. They had gathered around his truck while he loaded supplies into the specially designed compartments built into the bed. "There are a lot of reasons why steer contract red nose."

"Such as?" Reese asked.

Gabe doubted her interest stemmed from a desire to learn. She was fishing, attempting to discover if Gabe had overlooked the obvious.

"Improperly administered vaccines." The vet slammed shut the door of the last compartment. "Poor nutrition, for another. Young calves without proper feed and mineral supplements won't respond to the vaccination. Failure to administer booster vaccinations, though that's not the case here. The stress of transportation could have played a role. It weakens a steer's immune system." He leaned against the side of his truck, directing his comment at Reese. "And, sometimes, the vaccines plain don't work."

She didn't flinch. Gabe had seen her go head-to-head with his brothers and her ex-boyfriend Blake Nolan. During those occasions, he'd admired her fortitude and grit. Now he was on the receiving end, and he didn't like it.

"Is there anything more we can do?" Violet asked. "Other than quarantine the infected cattle and continue with an antibiotic regimen?"

The vet turned to face her. "All manner of supportive care. Rest, fluids, good food. Infectious bovine rhinotracheitis never goes away. It resides in the brain indefinitely. You can treat the symptoms, but not eradicate the disease."

They would have to reserve the rest of the hay for the sick cattle, who'd need more than the sporadic tufts of grass growing on the hills.

Dammit, thought Gabe. Another unplanned expense. Reese wouldn't let him hear the end of this.

"Can the steer still be sold?" she asked the vet.

"Absolutely. Once they've recovered."

"Can they get sick again?"

"You'll have to watch them closely." The vet presented Gabe with a handwritten bill. "I assume I give this to you."

"What about antibiotics?" Gabe spoke for the first time in a while. He'd been too stunned after the vet's devastating announcement to say much. "Can you leave us a supply and add them to the total?"

"Would if I could." The vet barely came up to Gabe's chin, yet he had a way of looming over people like a much taller man. "Don't have any extra. Not that I can sell you. Need to save all I have for my practice."

Gabe was momentarily confused. "What? Why?"

"There's a shortage of cattle antibiotics," the vet explained. "I have an order in. More should be arriving next week."

Pushing back his cowboy hat, Gabe rubbed his forehead where an irritating pain resided. "The steer are sick. I can't wait until next week."

"You could always try the feed store."

Gabe felt the pressure from all sides. Reese's eyes bored holes into his skull like twin laser beams. Violet chewed a thumbnail. His brothers spoke to each other in low, conspiratorial voices.

Refusing to succumb, Gabe reached in his pocket and removed the check he'd brought from the office. He filled in the invoice amount, using the hood of the truck for a desk.

"Appreciate the business," the vet said, accepting the check. "Merry Christmas."

"Same to you," Reese replied.

He saluted the group before leaving.

Only when he drove away did Gabe notice the wreath attached to the truck's tailgate and its blinking colored lights. The wreath made a mockery of his earlier feelings when it seemed as if his greatest wish was being granted. What an idiot he'd been.

Gabe headed for his truck.

Reese hurried after him. "Where are you going?"

Wasn't it obvious? "The feed store."

"I could come with you."

He stopped in his tracks and glared at her. "Why?"

She hesitated. "To keep you company."

"Are you sure you don't want to chew me out for my bad decision?"

"You couldn't know some of the steer were infected with red nose."

"But I am the one who convinced my brothers to purchase the herd and you to grant the draw on the line of credit."

"Gabe, I just want to help. Let me come with you."

Had he been too harsh on her? Misjudged her? "I need to stop at the house first for another check. Unless you refuse to cover it from the line of credit."

"I'll cover it."

She waited in the passenger seat while he went inside. They didn't speak much on the short drive to the center of town. Luckily, Ray's Feed Depot was open till six on Saturdays, giving them plenty of time. Perhaps they'd caught the spread of red nose before any significant damage was done. Gabe prayed that was the case.

Chapter 12

At the same moment Gabe and Reese approached the entrance to Ray's Feed Depot, the door swung wide and Blake Nolan stepped out, lugging a large cardboard box. He stopped, took note of them and nodded curtly. Did he remember seeing Gabe at the bank a few weeks ago?

"Reese. Gabe. How goes it?"

"Good." Reese didn't hesitate speaking first and, evidently, on behalf of Gabe.

"All right," Gabe added despite being far from all right. But Blake didn't need to know that. "How are your folks doing?"

"Keeping busy with the holidays. Thanks

for asking." Blake hesitated. "Sorry again about your dad. He was a fine man."

"Appreciate the kind words."

Blake and his wife, Wynonna, had come to the funeral. Gabe vaguely remembered seeing them among the throng of mourners.

"Well, take care." Blake nodded again, then left, the contents of the box rattling.

"Happy holidays," Reese said. By then Blake was long gone. She shrugged. "Clearly, he's still mad at me."

Gabe was more interested in what Blake was carrying. He swore the box contained bovine antibiotics. Was it a simple coincidence? Perhaps the vet had spread the news about Gabe's steer and the red nose outbreak. Yanking open the door, Gabe entered the feed store one step behind Reese. The life-size plastic horse just inside the entrance wore a wreath around its neck and a Santa hat on its head. Ray, the store's owner, dragged out the same tired decorations every year. Gabe paid them no mind. He was a man on a mission.

At the counter, he waited for Ray's niece and assistant manager, Alanna, to finish up with a customer.

"Hey, Gabe. Reese," she said when she was free. "What can I do for you?"

Several years older than Gabe, Alanna was short, plump and one of the hardest workers he'd ever seen. Without her, Ray would have been forced to sell the store when his son moved to Gila Bend last year.

Gabe leaned his elbows on the counter. Behind him, Reese waited, her booted foot tapping a staccato on the hardwood floor.

"We need all the bovine antibiotics you have in stock," he said, naming the brand the vet had recommended.

"Sure thing." Smiling pleasantly, Alanna disappeared through a door behind the counter. Gabe and everyone else who ever visited the store knew the supply room contained a large cooler where the medicines needing refrigeration were kept.

She returned a few minutes later, hugging five bottles to her chest, which she then set on the counter. Swiping her hands together, she asked, "Will that be all?"

He stared at the five bottles. "Where's the rest?"

"This is my entire supply."

"You're joking." He must have misheard, or she'd misunderstood him.

"Sorry. Blake Nolan bought up all our inventory but this. He heard there's been an outbreak of red nose in New Mexico and Texas and was stocking up before it traveled further west."

Gabe didn't clarify that the virus had already made its way to Mustang Valley. "What about a different brand?" The vet had mentioned other, less effective antibiotics that would do in a pinch.

Alanna shook her head. "Sorry. We're clean out of every kind."

"When will you get more in?"

"Next week." She then echoed what the vet had said. "Antibiotics are in short supply. Red nose is one of several respiratory outbreaks. This winter has been bad for cattle back East and in the Midwest, what with all the storms."

It was like a terrible dream from which there was no waking up. Buck Sadoski should have, but hadn't, mentioned the outbreak when he'd sold Gabe the steer. Buck had likely suspected, hence the low price.

Dammit! Gabe should have done his homework before agreeing to the sale. He'd heard about the storms. Who hadn't? It just hadn't registered. His oversight.

"Do you know where I can buy some?"

She scrunched her mouth to one side, thinking. "Let me call Rio Verde. They might have a supply." Alanna trotted over to the register and picked up a portable telephone handset. A minute later, she returned, her face saying it all. "Rio Verde is down to eleven bottles. If you want, they'll stay open an extra half hour."

Eleven bottles, plus these five, for thirty head of steer. That wouldn't last long. Nowhere near long enough to complete the number of days the vet had recommended Gabe treat the steer.

"You could always order online," Alanna suggested. "Might take a few days, assuming you find a supplier with enough product in stock."

What other choice did he have?

"Do you mind calling Rio Verde and letting them know I'm on my way?" He removed the check from his pocket.

"Tell me you aren't driving all the way to Rio Verde," Reese said, censure in her tone. They'd reached Gabe's truck, and she was opening the passenger door.

"I'll drop you home first," he said.

"I can ride with you."

"What about your dad?"

"He's resting. And Enrico's there."

Gabe handed her the paper sack of vaccine bottles to hold. "I don't need a babysitter."

"That's not the reason, Gabe."

"I'm going to save the steer. We won't lose the ranch."

"I know you're trying your best."

He bristled. More than censure, she was chastising him. "This could have happened to anyone."

"You're right." She adjusted the bottles more securely on her lap. He no sooner sat behind the wheel when she added, "But they may not be operating on a shoestring like you."

Here it comes, he thought, *the lecture*. Gabe jammed the key in the ignition.

"There's enough money left on the line of credit for the antibiotics, right?" he asked.

"You still have the artificial insemination to pay for. That's scheduled in a few days."

"We may have to impregnate fewer cows."

"May?" she asked.

He hastily threw the truck into Reverse and backed out of the parking space. "Don't patronize me."

She blew out a breath. "I deserve a share of the blame. I authorized the steer purchase even though I had my doubts."

"Except your livelihood's not on the line." And if it was, she still had her father and the Small Change to fall back on.

"It could be," she said, this time with noticeable worry in her voice.

Was it true? Could her job really be at stake? If so, Gabe would have more guilt to bear.

"Are you going to tell your brothers?" She glanced at him from across the seat.

"Yes."

"Today?"

"I'm well aware of my responsibilities, Reese. You don't have to keep nagging me."

She looked chagrined. "I'm sorry. I'm worried is all. Red nose is highly contagious."

He should be the one apologizing to her. "I didn't mean to snap at you."

"And I didn't mean to tell you what to do." She placed a hand on his leg. "We're in this together. Not just as business associates. I'm also your friend."

He had thought they were more than friends. He now realized they hadn't talked specifics, other than asking her to wait. His plans, his dreams, were simply that. *His*.

They reached a fork in the road. To the left was the Small Change. To the right, the road leading out of town and to Rio Verde. Unable to make a decision, Gabe stopped, letting the truck idle.

"Tell you what," Reese said, giving him an out. "Drop me at home. While you drive to Rio Verde, I'll find a supplier online and place the order."

After the way he'd treated her, that was far more than he deserved. "Thank you."

"I'll call when I have some information. Maybe I'll come by tomorrow and pick up Dad's horse."

Gabe would see to it General was fed and given a clean stall for the night.

He took the left fork. Moments later, he dropped off Reese at her doorstep.

"I can be there when you talk to your brothers," she offered almost shyly. "Give them the bank's perspective on the situation."

His first inclination was to utter a resounding no. On second thought, her presence might show his brothers that the bank supported Gabe and the purchase of the steer.

"I'll let you know when."

He wanted to kiss her. Heck, he always wanted to kiss her. But now, more than ever, they needed to maintain the professional boundaries they'd set. If things went badly and more steer contracted red nose, he didn't want either of them or their actions to come under question.

Apparently, Reese had fewer concerns than him, for she leaned across the seat and kissed his cheek tenderly before hopping out of the truck.

Gabe drove to Rio Verde as fast as the law allowed. Daylight was disappearing, and he needed to get there before the store closed.

As the desert scenery blurred by, he realized he was fighting for more than full ownership of Dos Estrellas. His future with Reese was also on the line and that was quickly becoming the most important reason to fight.

A thirty-seven-mile round-trip, practically wasted. Gabe sat at the kitchen table, drinking his midmorning coffee and fuming about his drive to Rio Verde the day before. By the time he arrived at the feed store, only five bottles were left. Ray's niece must have forgotten to call and say he was coming.

"I've never seen a shortage like this in all my fifteen years," the clerk had commented while ringing up the sale. "The weather back East is a killer."

Last night's news had shown the results of

another record-breaking storm—film footage of homes, cars and landmarks unrecognizable under piles of snow. Shipping services, hindered by the volume of holiday mailing, had stopped. Like Ray's Feed Depot, the store in Rio Verde wasn't getting a new supply of antibiotics for a week to ten days, if then.

Neither was Arizona immune from the harsh weather. Snow hammered the northern parts while heavy rain drenched central and southern areas. This morning, rain pelted the roof, causing a loud racket to fill the house. Sheets of water poured off the roof and flooded the courtyard, forming huge puddles outside the doors. The livestock pens and pastures had become muddy messes.

Gabe had been hoping and praying for just such a deluge. Now, he needed it to stop. The sick steer suffered worse in the cold and wet, and the healthy ones were more susceptible to infection.

Could his luck be any worse?

He, Violet and the two hands remaining at Dos Estrellas had risen at sunrise, donned their rain gear, and treated the infected steer. After that, they'd inspected the remaining herd for symptoms. They'd found three steer infected and moved them to section four.

As of late last night, Reese had yet to locate an online supplier. It was the same story everywhere. No antibiotics available until after Christmas. Perhaps not until the New Year. Since it was Sunday, most of the businesses were closed. The hunt had officially been put on hold.

Gabe briefly entertained the idea of delaying telling his brothers. They had some inkling of what was going on despite Gabe's efforts to keep them out of the loop. They weren't stupid.

Cole had gone to the Poco Dinero Saloon and Grill again last night, something he'd casually mentioned at breakfast. He'd heard the locals talking about the red nose outbreak in Texas and its swift move west to Arizona. If he'd said one word about the vet's visit yesterday, then half of Mustang Valley already suspected Dos Estrellas was in possession of infected steer.

To say the ranchers wouldn't be happy with Gabe was an understatement. If they suffered any losses because of red nose, he'd be vilified.

"Morning, *mijo*." Gabe's mother came up behind him and kissed the top of his head.

He absently patted her hand. "Hi, Mom."

"I thought, if you don't mind, I'd run into town and do some Christmas errands." With her brother Lorenzo definitely visiting for the holidays, she wanted to make sure they were well-stocked with his favorite foods.

"Of course I don't mind." Gabe drained the remainder of his coffee. "Where's Cara?"

"Visiting her mom. I hope Cara doesn't get stuck on the way home. You know how terrible traffic gets when it rains like this. Maybe I should call Leena's and tell Cara to stay the night."

Cara's mother had been a daily visitor at Dos Estrellas until she'd remarried and moved to Mesa a few years ago. Leena was more a sister than a friend to Raquel, and the reason Cara and her young son had moved to the ranch when she separated from her husband and stayed after the boy's death.

Gabe had contemplated asking Cara to be in on the talk with his brothers. Guess that wouldn't be happening now.

"Are you all right, *mijo*?" His mother sat down beside him, her smile a combination of affection and concern. "You seem distracted."

"I'm worried."

"It has been a difficult time for us."

"We're going to run out of antibiotics by tomorrow." Which was hardly his biggest problem. Feed remained in short supply, and they had almost no money for more.

"Something will come up. Reese is very smart." His mother's features softened. "I'm glad you two found each other."

Gabe tried to hide his reaction. "What are you talking about?"

"I'm your mother. I can see how you feel about her. And because I'm a woman, I can see how she feels about you. I approve. And your father would, too. He was right to pick her as his trustee."

"Wait a minute. Are you saying Dad picked Reese because he wanted us to hook up?"

"Of course not. He picked her because she was Theo's daughter."

"That makes no sense."

"Ah, but it does." She tapped the side of her head and winked. "Think about it. Your father wanted his will carried out to the letter and knew Reese would work extra hard to ensure there wasn't the slightest deviation."

"Because she's Theo McGraw's daughter."

"And because she's very good at her job. She wouldn't want to be accused of any… What is the word? Yes, improprieties."

Gabe could see the logic, though it was

slightly skewed, in his opinion, and hurtful. "Dad trusted a person he hardly knew, a person who could well ruin the ranch, more than me."

"No, no, *mijo*."

"Funny thing is, I'm not sure Dad was wrong." Gabe thought of himself purchasing the sick steer, rushing headlong into a decision and thinking only of himself. "He was a lot wiser than any of us gave him credit for."

"He was worried his sons would fight."

"He had good reason to worry."

She sighed, more wistful than sad. "Your father and I made mistakes. We were young and in love. Even so, it wasn't fair to his wife. I don't blame her for being angry and for passing her anger on to her sons."

She rarely spoke of his father's ex-wife. Now that Gabe thought about it, the two women must have crossed paths. Both had lived in Mustang Valley for a number of years. Surely, they'd run into each other at the market or the Holly Daze Festival. How would his father's ex-wife have felt, confronting her husband's mistress?

For the first time in his life, Gabe felt sorry for Josh and Cole's mother. She must have been deeply wounded by his dad. Which didn't justify her turning her sons against their father, but it did explain a lot.

Was that why Blake didn't acknowledge Celia? To protect his wife, their marriage and their sons?

"Your father's last wish was for you and your brothers to reconcile." His mother's voice penetrated his thoughts. "It wasn't possible while he was alive because Josh and Cole's mother refused to allow it. Now there's a chance. If you are willing."

Gabe wished he was a bigger person, one with more forgiveness in his heart. "I'm not sure I am. They knew Dad was dying, and they didn't come out. Not until Hector called them and told them they were named as beneficiaries in Dad's will."

"You assume it's greed that brought them here."

"Isn't it?"

"Their mother's parents have money, and they'll probably inherit a portion."

"Maybe they didn't want to wait or they aren't on good terms. Josh didn't ask his grandparents to help with his attorney costs when he was fighting for custody of his kids."

"I don't care what brought them here."

Raquel's voice grew higher. "I'm glad they're staying. For your father and for you."

"Why for me?"

"You've felt all your life you weren't as good as them."

"Not true."

"It is." His mother gazed at him earnestly. "It's also true you're every bit as good as them and were loved by your father as much, if not more. Them being here will show you."

Gabe doubted that, but his mother could have a point. He was the son raised by his father his entire life. The one taught by him. Given his love. Not his brothers. Their anger and resentment might be because they didn't think they were as good as Gabe. It was something to ponder.

"I have to talk to them about the sick steer and our chances. It looks bleak, Mom."

"How bleak?"

"We're in trouble."

She stood and kissed the top of his head again. "You'll figure this out. You and Reese."

Her optimism was sweet. And naive. They were in for the battle of their lives.

His cell phone rang, and Gabe answered it, noting Reese's number. "Hello."

"I don't have good news," she blurted.

He propped an elbow on the table and rested his forehead in his hand. "You didn't find any online suppliers with antibiotics."

"None of them will promise a shipment until after Christmas. And that isn't all."

He didn't like the tone in her voice. "What?"

"Because of the shortage, prices are sky-rocketing. Whatever supply we get our hands on will cost us top dollar."

Their situation was worse than yesterday.

"Okay." What else was there to say? Realistically, he'd expected this. Deep inside, he had hoped for more.

"What time did you want me over there?" Reese asked.

The meeting with his brothers, the one she was planning on attending. He'd momentarily forgotten.

"After lunch. One o'clock."

"It's going to work out," Reese said.

"I'm not sure how." With his mother nearby, he didn't dare say anything personal, even though she had correctly surmised he and Reese were involved. "See you soon," he said and disconnected.

"Not good news?" His mother came over when he'd disconnected from Reese.

He explained the situation, unable to hide

his disappointment. "If I could put off talking to Josh and Cole, I would."

"Don't." His mother shook her head. "Your father would expect you to do what's right and take charge."

"Please stop defending him, Mom," Gabe bit out. "I loved Dad and hate that he died, but let's be honest. He really screwed things up. For all of us. You said so yourself."

"I'm not defending him." She sounded hurt. "I'm supporting you. I don't doubt for one second you will find the answers necessary to save Dos Estrellas."

She said *the answers* as if a red nose outbreak was no more serious than a skin rash.

"We have to face facts."

"*You* must have *faith*," she said before walking away.

Faith? They needed a miracle. For the skies to clear, the grass to grow, the steer to recover and at least eight hundred healthy calves born next year.

Rather than his spirits lifting, Gabe experienced the weight of his mistake pushing him further and further down. He might well be buried under one of those piles of snow he'd seen on the news last night.

Chapter 13

Normally, the land between the horse barn and the ranch house was dry as dust. When the rain fell in torrents, like today, the shallow wash filled with water within a matter of hours. It now resembled a raging river ten feet wide.

Two years ago, Gabe's father had crossed in the quad and inadvertently flooded the engine, resulting in hundreds of dollars' worth of damage. Several times, when Gabe had been young and foolhardy, he'd daringly waded into the running wash, only to be swept away in the muddy water and carried a hundred feet before gaining his footing.

This afternoon, he wasn't so careless and crossed at the lowest point. It was a slow, arduous process, made more uncomfortable by his silently fuming brothers in the truck's rear seat. Violet sat beside him and, every few seconds, cast him a concerned look.

Moments ago, the four of them had come in from checking the herd yet again. More sick steer were discovered, bringing the total to over forty.

Gabe alternately looked out the side window at the rushing water and ahead, through the windshield, at the bank on the other side. Rain slammed the glass and, combined with the swiftly thumping wipers, hampered his vision. Finally, the truck bumped and rocked as the front wheels climbed out of the water and onto solid ground. He heard a collective sigh of relief from his passengers.

A five-foot-high slatted fence surrounded the house and yard, separating it from the horse stables, cattle barn, livestock pens, hay sheds and other outbuildings. Gabe rolled slowly through the gate and spotted Reese's car in the driveway. He pulled up beside her vehicle and shut off the truck. All four doors simultaneously opened, and everyone piled out. The flaps of Gabe's unfastened rain slicker blew open. He ignored the rain that pelted him, stinging his skin through his shirt and jeans, and soaking him to the bone.

At the back door, they stomped the water and muck from their boots and removed their slickers before entering the mudroom. They wiped their boots with rags before entering the house. Gabe's mother wouldn't be happy if they tracked dirt and water on her clean floors.

She'd opted out of the meeting, though Gabe had wanted her to attend. She'd claimed her presence might make his brothers uncomfortable and unwilling to express their opinions. She had fresh coffee waiting for them on the counter. Chai tea for Violet. They each grabbed a mug and a handful of Christmas sugar cookies.

Reese sat in the dining room at the end of the table, holding a steaming mug. She glanced up as they entered the room. A musical, motion-activated Christmas tree on the buffet began playing "Jingle Bells."

Everyone stood stonily for the next ten seconds. After the music stopped, they sat.

"Quite the rain we're having," Reese addressed to no one in particular.

"It's supposed to continue until tomorrow," Violet remarked.

Complete silence. No one was in the mood for small talk.

Gabe's gaze wandered the table. He was reminded of Thanksgiving dinner, the last time they had all been in this room together. That gathering had ended badly, with Josh and Cole storming out. Would this one end the same? Studying his brothers' stern faces, he decided the odds were in favor of it. They hadn't appreciated Gabe putting off their questions about the sick steer.

"Shall we begin?" Reese deferred to Gabe.

He'd thought of little else all morning except this meeting, even mentally rehearsing what he'd say. Now that the moment had arrived, his preparation deserted him.

"You may have figured out we're dealing with a bovine virus outbreak," he began. "It's called red nose and over forty of our steer are affected."

"Is it fatal?" Josh asked.

"No."

"How did they contract it?" Cole demanded.

"Some of the steer were sick when we bought them."

"Didn't you check?"

"Gabe took every precaution," Reese insisted. "This could have happened to anyone."

Cole's eyes narrowed. "But it happened to us."

Gabe didn't rise to the bait Cole dangled, though he wanted to. Badly. "Between the snow storms back East and bovine virus outbreaks across the country, we're having trouble buying the necessary antibiotics." He paused. "We, all of us, need to decide a course of action."

"What do you suggest?" Josh asked.

Gabe evaluated his older brother, searching for clues to his frame of mind. "Continue our attempts to purchase antibiotics at the best available price. Inspect the herd twice a day and quarantine the sick steer. Feed them what's left of the supplemental hay and grain. Watch our other cattle for signs and isolate them if necessary."

"Quarantining is especially important," Reese added. "It's imperative we stop the red nose from spreading."

He'd been about to say the same thing. Coming from Reese, it smacked of criticism. He shifted uncomfortably.

"It would be best to get the cattle out of the

rain," he said. "But we have no facility capable of accommodating that many sick steer."

Dos Estrellas had a cattle barn—a two-thousand-square-foot pen covered by a metal awning—but it was small, rundown and sorely inadequate for housing forty-plus head of sick steer.

Of the two original cattle barns, one had fallen to dry rot five years ago. Gabe's father hadn't gotten around to replacing it, mostly due to lack of money. The other cattle barn was on the land dedicated to Cara's mustang sanctuary and used for her horses.

"I was at the Poco Dinero Saloon and Grill the other night," Cole said. "Everyone was talking about the red nose outbreak."

"Your point?" Gabe asked.

"The ranchers are having some big pow-wow Tuesday night at the community center."

Gabe frowned. "I haven't heard anything."

"Just repeating the talk."

He was tempted to check his phone to see if he'd missed a call or text during their hectic day. Wait. What if the local ranchers didn't want to include him in the meeting because they believed he was responsible for bringing red nose to Mustang Valley? Or, maybe they didn't see him as the owner of Dos Estrellas.

A swig of coffee didn't alleviate the bad taste in his mouth.

"What's the worst that can happen?" Josh asked with far less attitude than his brother. "We need to be prepared."

"The infection spreads," Gabe said blandly. "We lose steer."

"How many?"

"Between the lack of antibiotics and the foul weather, it could be five, ten percent. More if any other cattle become infected."

"Can we recover from that?"

"Possibly. Probably," he amended. "As long as we can inseminate the cows as planned and they don't get sick."

"What if they do?"

Gabe, Reese and Violet all exchanged glances. Red nose was hardest on pregnant cows.

"They'll likely miscarry," Violet said.

"Great." Cole spat out a bitter laugh.

"There's still the mustang sanctuary." Josh said. "If we had the five hundred acres, we could use the cattle barn and extra grazing land for isolating the sick steer."

"Nothing's changed." Gabe should have anticipated this question and was mad that he hadn't. "We'd have to find a place for the horses."

"Why not sell them? We could use the money to buy antibiotics."

"Two hundred horses?"

"Only enough for the cash we need to carry us through."

Gabe shook his head. "Sale proceeds have always gone back into the sanctuary."

"Didn't Cara get money from the fund drive during the Holly Daze Festival?"

"She has a lot of horses to feed."

"Have you asked her?" Josh's demeanor changed with each question, going from civil to insistent to impatient to irritated.

Gabe's own irritation was rising. "I doubt we could sell the horses in time to make a difference. She has a detailed adoption process, matching the horse to the potential owner."

"You didn't answer my question."

"I have not asked her. Nor will I."

"Then, by all means, allow me."

"Stay away from Cara." Gabe was glad she was visiting her mother. He wouldn't have wanted her to witness how little his brothers cared.

"If you lose the ranch," Reese said, "she and your mom lose their home."

Gabe faced her. "You think I don't know that?"

"Josh's suggestion has merit."

"I thought you liked Cara."

Reese jerked as if affronted. "I do. Very much. But, as the trustee of your father's estate, I have to put the ranch first. Losing it will greatly affect your mother and Cara, who might be willing to help by selling some horses."

"No one buys a horse over Christmas."

"You didn't get a pony for a gift when you were a kid?" Cole asked.

"She could advertise them as Christmas presents," Violet added.

"That's not a bad idea," Reese remarked thoughtfully.

Gabe hated the satisfied expressions on his brothers' faces. This shouldn't be a contest, yet it felt like one, and Reese was choosing sides.

He tried telling himself she was being impartial; her job at the bank dictated nothing less. But her agreeing with Josh hit him like an invisible sucker punch to the sternum. He and Reese had kissed. Expressed their growing feelings for each other. Shared secrets and private wishes. Discussed a potential future relationship when the time was right.

And while he understood, the invisible blow still stunned him.

"Isn't it your responsibility to ensure my father's plan is carried out?" he asked her.

"Of course."

"Well, his plan included Cara keeping the mustang sanctuary."

"For as long as she wants it. She may choose differently, in light of the red nose epidemic."

"You can't really think that. Her son died. The sanctuary is all she has. I won't ask her to give it up."

"Like I said," Josh interceded. "I'll do it."

Gabe didn't realize he was standing until the musical Christmas tree started playing "Santa Claus is Coming to Town."

"Gabe, please sit down," Reese said.

He ignored her.

Reese ignored him and addressed his brothers. "There are other solutions than closing the mustang sanctuary or selling horses. We should explore those, too."

Take the higher road, Gabe's father and Reese had both advised. If he stormed out of the room, he would gain nothing and likely lose considerable ground.

"I'm listening."

He sat at the same time the musical Christmas tree stopped playing. Good thing, because he was ready to throw it across the room.

Reese had worked in the banking business for over six years. In that time, she'd seldom panicked. Today was one of those rare occasions. Gabe and his brothers didn't agree on anything and insisted on battling. It was her job to mediate, offer ideas and guide them in the right direction.

Frankly, she didn't know if she was capable of it. And if she failed...

No, not an option.

"The insurance settlement your mother received," Josh said to Gabe. "She could float us a loan."

"Forget it. My father took out that policy so she'd have a nest egg."

"You're right." Josh placed his palms on the table top and breathed deeply. "Because she's going to need the money when we lose the ranch."

Gabe clenched his teeth, then forced himself to breathe evenly. "Funny how every solution you come up with involves my family giving up what Dad left them. What are you willing to give up?"

"Now wait a minute," Cole snapped.

"Don't tell me you're broke. Your grandparents are loaded."

Josh's head snapped up. "We're not asking my grandparents for money."

"But I'm supposed to ask my family."

Reese had reached her limit—for the third time. "Your mother may want to lend you the money."

Gabe gawked at her.

"You should at least ask her."

"Me," he stated flatly.

"You did buy the infected steer," Cole reminded him.

Before Gabe could retaliate, Reese interrupted.

"This is every bit my fault as Gabe's. I authorized the draw on the line of credit."

"But you don't have to bear the consequences," Josh stated.

"My position at the bank could come under examination."

Cole stared at her hard. "When you authorized the draw, is it possible your judgment was affected by your relationship with Gabe?"

She'd wondered when this question would be asked and by whom.

"Gabe and I are friends." Not a lie. "Nothing more." An exaggeration. "We agreed to maintain a strictly professional relationship." The honest truth.

She shot Gabe the briefest of glances and was surprised to see his features harden. Wasn't that what they'd agreed on?

"I've heard a different version around town," Cole said.

Probably at the Poco Dinero Saloon and Grill. Reese swore men were worse gossips than women.

"You have nothing to worry about in that regard," she assured him.

He grunted indifferently.

"I authorized the draw because you three were in agreement and the price for the steer was very good. You could have said no. You could also have done more research before agreeing, possibly learning about the spread of red nose."

Cole nodded and he sat back. "I did agree. And it's a decision I hope I don't regret."

"What about our immediate plans?" Josh asked, his demeanor also less antagonistic.

Reese squared her shoulders. "I suggest we wait a week, until after Christmas. If the steer don't improve, then we sell off the healthy ones, using the money to pay the most pressing bills, buy antibiotics when they become available and supplemental feed for the remaining cattle."

"Should we talk to Raquel and Cara?"

"Let's revisit that next week. It won't make much difference before then, and why ruin the holidays? The steer could improve, after all."

She wished she sounded more convincing.

"There's one more solution we haven't discussed," Cole said tersely. "Selling the ranch."

Gabe slammed the table causing Violet to jump. "That's always your answer. Sell the ranch and get your share of the money so you can leave."

Reese hoped Gabe kept his raging emotions under control. To help, she delivered her next words calmly and rationally. "Selling may be a little premature."

"At the rate we're going," Cole said, "we could lose everything."

"We have weeks, if not months, to spare. And other solutions to try first."

Gabe pushed back from the table, setting off the musical Christmas tree again. He shot it a dirty look before turning that look on Cole. "You agreed to stay in Mustang Valley and work the ranch for a year."

"I did. Before you set out to ruin us by buying sick steer."

"Set out?"

"Why not? For all I know, you could have misled Josh and me on purpose."

"What would that have gotten me?"

"You want us gone."

"No fooling."

The Christmas tree finally stopped playing. Reese stood, picked up the tree and activated the off switch.

She faced the table and planted her hands on her hips. "The purpose of this meeting was to discuss viable options for the immediate future. Not pick fights with each other."

The three men quieted. She allowed herself a small sigh.

"Unless someone has a better idea, then I vote we wait a week and reassess the situation after Christmas. In the meanwhile, we focus all efforts on the sick steer."

"I assume we're done here." Cole pushed to his feet.

"Unless you have any objections."

Avoiding eye contact with each other, the three brothers exited the room. Violet followed, giving Reese a one-shoulder shrug.

She sagged into her chair. The last thirty minutes had been stressful. Rousing herself, she headed for the kitchen, the direction Gabe had taken. She assumed he'd be waiting for her and was surprised to find the kitchen empty.

Reese returned to the dining room, gathered up her briefcase, coat, umbrella and purse, turned on the musical Christmas tree then left out the front door.

Gabe waited for her by her car, his face unreadable. He'd donned his jacket and cowboy hat, which he'd pushed low on his head to ward off the rain and not, she assumed, to look tough.

Something told her he wasn't in the mood for a friendly chat. Nevertheless, she smiled in greeting.

"Hi."

He nodded in return.

She stopped at her car, holding the umbrella over them both. Water pooled at their feet. "I know the meeting didn't go exactly as you wanted."

"Exactly?"

His sharp retort put her on the defense. "I was doing my job, Gabe. And from what I could tell, it went reasonably well. The decision to wait a week is a good one."

"I'm not arguing your decision."

She lifted her chin. "Is that what we're doing? Arguing?"

"You know how important the sanctuary is to Cara and how much my mother needs the insurance money."

"And you heard Cole in there. I can't, *we can't*, allow our romantic involvement for each other to affect our judgment or give anyone a reason to think it is."

He visibly bristled. "I couldn't have said it better myself."

She wasn't stupid. Something more was going on with Gabe than residual anger after the meeting. "Why were you waiting for me?"

"I still have no idea what there was between us other than a few kisses."

His remark stung. "It was more than that. Was I wrong?"

"You're the trustee of my father's will."

"For now. But later, when—"

"Not later," he said. "Not ever. I think today proved it."

The wind tugged at her umbrella, and she gripped the handle harder, feeling a little unsteady. "I don't understand."

Gabe shook his head and, for the first time, she noted the hurt in his dark eyes. "I'm not the man for you, Reese. I never was. And I was stupid to think we had a chance."

"Stupid?" Was that what he thought? Her chest hurt, more when she tried to draw a deep breath. "My mistake. I thought you cared about me."

"It's not going to work. You're Theo McGraw's daughter."

"That's not why I sided with your brothers."

"So, you admit it."

"No. I was…" She faltered, struggled. "Let's wait until after Christmas to continue this conversation. You're worried about the sick steer. Once they improve, you'll feel different about us."

"I won't."

"I see." She had her pride and refused to beg.

"I alone am to blame for buying the sick steer," he said.

"Not true. Me, your brothers—"

"It's completely true. And Cole was right about what he said in the meeting, only he had it backwards. I let my feelings for you affect my judgment."

"I don't agree."

"I was gung ho to buy the steer because I thought I could turn a quick profit."

"There's nothing wrong with that, Gabe. It was a business decision."

"So I could buy out my brothers."

"Which would make them happy. And you, too."

"I also did it because the sooner I got sole ownership of the ranch, the sooner you and I could start seeing each other."

"None of those are bad reasons."

"I could lose everything important to me." His voice changed. Deepened. "Because I wanted you."

"Quit being so hard on yourself." She was losing him. She could feel it, and her heart started breaking.

"Will you be saying the same thing when we're selling what little is left of the ranch?" He shut his eyes. "It was a mistake. All of it."

"Not all of it. There were some incredible moments." She reached for him, but her hand fell short.

"I think you should leave."

Her lower lip trembled. Dammit, she wasn't like prone to tears. She was strong, and had been that way since her mother left. The night of her senior prom, when Gabe had held her, was one of the few times she'd allowed herself to cry.

She fumbled for the car door handle.

Gabe didn't stop her. Why would he?

She snapped closed her umbrella, practically dropping it as she slid into the car. Before she could close the door, Gabe bent low, one hand resting on the roof.

"I'm sorry," he said.

"Me, too." Despite her best efforts, her voice shook.

He stepped back. She shut the door and drove away.

God, how could she have made such a mess of things? She'd fallen for him. Gabe Dempsey. The most inappropriate man in all of Mustang Valley.

She didn't cry on the ride home. Silent tears streaming down her cheeks didn't count. Neither did quiet sobs. Crying wasn't real unless a person made noise.

That was what she told herself, anyway.

The moment she walked in the house, her father confronted her.

He took one look at her and pulled her into his embrace. "What happened, sweetie?"

Her reply was to make noise. Lots and lots of it as she cried hard enough to soak the front of his shirt.

Chapter 14

"That's the last of it, boss." Violet swiped her palms down her coat, brushing away the bits and pieces of hay clinging to her.

Gabe wondered how long she'd be calling him boss, then supposed it didn't matter. The name had lost its shine, the result of his short and disastrous run in charge of Dos Estrellas.

"What do you think?" he asked.

"We have enough hay for a few more days."

He'd been inquiring about the health of the steer, not the feed supply, but he could see how Violet made the leap. She and Gabe had just finished unloading a truck bed full of hay into the metal feeders, one on each end of the barn. The sick cattle, moving lethargically, vied for available space around the feeders. The fact they had an appetite at all was heartening.

"On the plus side," Violet continued, "the grass is making a comeback."

Good news indeed. The recent rains had worked their magic. Three days since the torrent, three days since his meeting with Reese and his brothers, and new shoots of grass could be seen poking up from the ground, encouraged by the shining sun and sudden warm spell.

Unfortunately, growing grass was the *only* good news. They had run out of antibiotics two days ago, after moving twenty-five of the sickest steer to the undersized cattle barn. Their inspection of the herd this morning had added six more infected steer, bringing the grand total to fifty-three.

Quarantining helped but not enough. Like humans, cattle were contagious for one or two days before displaying any symptoms. By then, the virus had continued its destructive rampage through the herd.

A larger cattle barn might make a difference. Like the one in the mustang sanctuary. Gabe refused to ask Cara. He might still refuse at the end of the week. Yesterday, Josh had remarked about them missing the opportunity to sell mustangs as Christmas gifts. Gabe had walked away in disgust, mostly at himself. He'd been thinking the same thing.

He'd also been thinking Reese was right to support Josh's suggestions. His mother and Cara deserved a say in the decisions and an opportunity to assist if they chose. Excluding them was unfair.

On the other hand, putting undue pressure on them was also unfair.

Reese was on his mind a lot. All day, all night. He regretted blindsiding her after the family meeting. It wasn't nice. Telling himself that a quick and clean breakup was best didn't alleviate his guilt. He felt precisely like the heel he was. He'd made the right decision, spared her from losing her heart to, and subsequently being hurt by, a guy completely wrong for her. It was his execution that stank.

"As least these fellows aren't getting any sicker." Violet patted a steer's brown rump through the railing.

"Yeah." Try as he might, Gabe couldn't muster any enthusiasm.

There were still the cattle in the pastures to consider. More could be coming down with red nose. The last of the line of credit was slated for the antibiotics due to arrive on the twenty-eighth—if the shipment wasn't delayed. Snowstorms back East were finally easing and shipping services resuming.

Hopefully, they could hold out until then. Less than a single tower of hay remained from the additional supply they'd purchased. Then again, if steer started dying, supplementing the feed would no longer be a problem.

Gabe was glad none of the other ranches were affected with red nose, and that he hadn't been run out of town. At the community center last night, the other ranchers had sympathized. It was a small consolation.

"I have something to tell you," Violet said, her manner reserved. "If you don't mind."

"Fire away."

"Whatever happens, I want you to know what a good job you've done."

He almost laughed. "You're in the minority."

"No, really. It can't be easy, and you've stepped up, Gabe. A lot more than your bro—" She winced. "Sorry, but that's my opinion."

He smiled. "Thanks for the support. It means a lot."

"We're going to get through this, boss."

"I hope you're right."

"Rest assured, you're stuck with me till the bitter end."

Smiling for the first time all day, Gabe pushed off the fence. "Come on. Let's get out of here."

A late model pickup traveling the narrow dirt road behind the horse pastures had them pausing. It turned onto the property and headed straight for them. Gabe didn't recognize the vehicle. Then he spotted the occupants. What in the world?

Enrico, the Small Change's livestock manager, pulled up alongside Gabe's truck and cut the engine. He and Theo McGraw emerged, Theo with some difficulty. Planting his feet on the ground, he used a cane to steady himself.

Gabe stepped forward, ready to assist if necessary.

Theo dismissed him. "I'm fine."

"Of course."

"Young lady." He spoke pleasantly to Violet. "Would you be kind enough to give us a minute?"

"Yes, sir." She glanced at Gabe, then backed away. After a brief, uncertain pause, she made for the Small Change truck.

She and Enrico met up at the tailgate where they began conversing.

Gabe studied Theo for a moment. How much did he know about Gabe and Reese, and was this unexpected visit related?

"What can I do for you?"

"I'm thinking, it's what I can do for you. I understand you're fighting a red nose break-out."

Theo hadn't been at the community center last evening, but had obviously heard the news from Reese.

"I am." Gabe was curious. This was no casual visit.

"I can help. I have a supply of antibiotics." Theo hobbled toward the fence, leaning heavily on his cane, his gait unsteady. "You're welcome to them."

Gabe chuckled. "I need a lot."

"I have over two hundred bottles."

Wow. That was more than enough to carry Dos Estrellas through until their shipment arrived.

"We've placed an order," Gabe said. "Should be here on the twenty-eighth. But, if you're offering, I'd like to buy fifty bottles from you."

"Take it all."

"I won't leave you in a lurch." The outbreak could hit the Small Change.

"Fine. But it's there if you need it."

"Thank you." Gabe was grateful. And overwhelmed by Theo's generosity. Removing his cowboy hat, he knocked it against his thigh, needing a moment to compose himself.

"Come by whenever you're ready," Theo said. "No cost. You can replace what you've used when your supply arrives."

Gabe couldn't accept the offer without first knowing the reason for it. "Why are you doing this?"

"Isn't it enough we're neighbors and should look out for each other?"

"You and my father were rivals."

"He would have done no less for me."

Gabe could easily see his father helping Theo in a crisis.

"But that's not the reason I'm offering you my supply of antibiotics." The older man smiled. "It's Reese."

Gabe said nothing, unsure how to explain what had transpired between him and Reese or how much to reveal. Theo should be reading Gabe the riot act, given he'd hurt his daughter, not offering him his precious supply of antibiotics. "About that…"

"You didn't have to keep Reese's secret all these years, but you did."

"Secret?"

"Don't play dumb. I know she had a baby."

Gabe's jaw dropped. He hadn't been this thrown for a loop since kissing Reese in the garage. "She told you?"

"No, though I wish she had." Theo seemed to lose himself in memories. "I gave her a difficult time when she set her sights on Blake Nolan, though I blamed him more than I did her. He was engaged. And older. In college. He took advantage of her naivety."

"When did you find out?" Gabe asked.

Theo leaned against the fence, his left leg trembling slightly. He absently rubbed it with his free hand. "Right before her high school graduation. I'd suspected something was going on for a few weeks."

That would have been about the time of Gabe and Reese's senior prom. Theo was clearly astute. Or, he loved his daughter and paid attention to her.

"She spent a lot of time in her room on the phone," Theo continued. "I became concerned. One afternoon, she thought I wasn't home. I heard her talking to her cousin Megan. They were making plans." He paused. "When she told me she wanted to take a year off before college and stay with Megan, I pretended I didn't know her real reasons. I agreed with her decision to give up the baby and figured she'd tell me when she was ready. She hasn't yet." His voice grew husky.

"She loves you, sir," Gabe said. "She didn't want to disappoint you."

Theo turned misty eyes on Gabe. "She couldn't if she tried."

"Maybe you should tell her and not me."

"Maybe I should." The older man studied Gabe. "You're pretty smart. Like your dad."

"I consider that a compliment."

"I owe you for protecting Reese."

"You don't owe me a thing, Theo." Gabe had never called his neighbor by anything other than Mr. McGraw. Using his first name felt right under the circumstances. "Certainly not your supply of antibiotics. It was my honor to help Reese. I… I care about her."

"The feeling's mutual, I assure you."

"Did she say anything?"

"No. But I know my daughter. She's quite smitten with you."

"She is?" The news pleased Gabe, though it shouldn't. He'd made it clear they had no future.

"Treat her well, or you'll have me to deal with."

"Actually, Theo, we're not involved."

"A situation you can easily remedy."

"Things aren't that simple."

"No?" His mouth curved in an amused smile.

Admitting one's shortcomings was never easy. "I don't have anything to offer her," Gabe said. "My family's on the brink of losing the ranch. Buried in debt. Fighting a red nose epidemic."

"You love her, don't you?"

Did he? Was there ever a question? "Yes."

"Then it is simple."

"I can't go to her until I have more to offer."

Theo scratched his bristled jaw. "You'll pull through this, son, and when you do, I expect you to make my daughter happy."

It was a pipe dream. "I imagine that's going to take some time."

"Then I suppose you should get after it." He started for his truck. "I'll see you shortly. When you pick up the antibiotics."

"Thank you again."

The older man kept walking. "Reese usually gets home from work about five-thirty."

Enrico appeared from behind the truck to open the passenger door. Theo waved him off.

Violet hurried to join Gabe. "Well?"

"I'll fill you in later."

She accepted his answer without comment.

He'd go to the Small Change today. Whether he arrived before Reese got home or afterward would depend on how the conversation with his family went.

Because of Theo's generosity, they had a chance. A slim one, but a chance. The rest was up to them.

Gabe and Violet arrived at the horse stables and he noticed two things—an unfamiliar truck and livestock trailer departing the ranch and Cole in the round pen, working a horse on a lunge line. Not just any horse, one of Cara's mustangs.

Gabe looked at Violet. That made no sense. His younger brother hadn't shown the slightest interest in the mustangs or the sanctuary, other than reclaiming the land for the cattle operation.

They strode over to the round pen. Josh was also watching his brother and turned at their approach.

"Afternoon." He tugged on the brim of his hat.

"What's going on?" Gabe asked.

Violet squeezed past the two men and rested her forearms on the railing.

Josh hitched a thumb at his brother. "Cole's

working with one of Cara's more promising horses."

Gabe had always conceded his younger brother had a way with horses, and he was showing it now. Or showing off. The horse, a young, green broke gelding with a stubborn streak and flashy markings, had been testing Cara's patience for months. Yet, he responded to Cole's cues to walk, trot and lope on command like a docile lesson mount.

"Since when is he interested in training mustangs?" Gabe said.

Josh didn't take his eyes off Cole. "He's going to need a new saddle horse."

"What? He has four horses."

"Not any more. He sold them."

The unfamiliar truck and trailer Gabe had seen leaving. "Why?"

"He has his reasons."

None that made any sense to Gabe. "What's going on here?"

Cole tugged on the lunge line and commanded the horse to walk, then stand. The horse obediently halted, snorting and shaking his handsome head from side to side. Cole unhooked the lunge line from the halter. He gave the horse a friendly scratching between the ears before shooing him away.

"Get along, boy."

The horse trotted a few feet, stopped at the railing and hung his head over the side, no longer interested in the humans.

Gabe met Cole at the round pen gate. "Why did you sell your roping horses?"

He expected attitude from Cole. He didn't get it.

"I don't need them."

"You're going to quit rodeoing?"

"For now." Cole shut the gate, leaving the young mustang on his own.

Gabe was flabbergasted. "You're not making any sense." He stepped in front of Cole, blocking his path.

"I was going to tell you later." Cole shrugged.

"Tell me now."

Cole removed a small folded piece of paper from his coat pocket. He gave it to Gabe.

"What's this?"

"A check. I figured we could use the money for another couple truckloads of hay and inseminating the cows. Don't want to miss breeding season altogether."

Gabe opened the check. Seeing the amount, he swallowed. "You had them make it out to the ranch."

"Easier to deposit."

He pushed the check back at Cole. "We don't need this."

"We do, brother."

Brother? He'd never called Gabe that before. "I don't understand."

Cole leaned his back against the round pen railing. Josh and Violet remained nearby, waiting expectantly.

"I'm a man of my word," Cole said. "When I make a commitment, I commit. Fully. I told you I'd give the ranch a year."

"Right." Gabe didn't believe him.

"If we lose Dos Estrellas because of the sick steer or a shortage of feed, I won't have given you a full year."

"If we lose the ranch, you get your share of the money and an excuse to leave. Without having to sell your horses." Gabe hadn't known until he saw the check just how much championship roping horses were worth.

"Who says I want to leave?" Cole's attention on Gabe didn't waver.

"It's all you've talked about."

"Josh needs a place to bring his kids next month."

All right. Gabe could buy that reason a little more. The two brothers were thick as thieves. Still....

"Why not give Josh the money?"

"He wouldn't take it," Cole answered off-handedly.

That was likely true. Josh was a proud man. A quality he probably inherited from their father. Like Gabe. When all was said and done, hadn't his battle with his brothers for the ranch really been a matter of pride?

"The only way I can make sure my niece and nephew have a home," Cole continued, "is to help pull this ranch out of the hole we've dug."

"You didn't dig the hole."

"I did." For the first time, Cole spoke without a giant chip on his shoulder. "I agreed to buy the steer. I did it for one reason. I wanted gone from this place as fast as I could get away. I made a bad decision that affected everyone in this family."

Gabe had recently said almost the same thing to Reese about himself. He, too, had let personal feelings affect his judgment.

"Still not your fault." He hoped no one noticed the slight crack in his voice. It had been an emotional day.

"You're splitting hairs." Cole put a hand on Gabe's shoulder. His grip was almost affectionate. "Buy the hay and get the cows bred.

Let's make it through the holidays and the next month or two."

Gabe fingered the check. He could refuse. Tear it up and let the breeze carry the pieces away. Or he could take the check and put it to good use.

Cole had sold his most precious possessions to help the ranch *and* the family, which included Gabe's mother and Cara. His actions showed he was willing to put his resentment aside for the good of all. Gabe could do no less.

He stuffed the check into his jacket pocket—and felt a weight lift from him.

Theo and Cole, the two people Gabe least expected, had offered the greatest help. Dos Estrellas wasn't out of the woods yet, but a path lay ahead. Cole smiled. Josh was smiling, too, as was Violet. But she had tears in her eyes.

"You going to stand there like a lump on log?" Cole asked, "Or go inside and make a call to the hay company?"

"I have someone to see first." Gabe hadn't realized he'd made a decision until the words were out.

"Let me guess." Cole grinned. "Reese."

He considered telling his brothers about the

antibiotics, then decided it could wait. He had something more pressing to do first.

"I'll see you at dinner." His glance took in Cole and Josh. His brothers. His family. There was a nice ring to it.

On impulse, he shook Cole's hand and then Josh's. They responded enthusiastically.

"Take your time," Josh said as Gabe hurried to his truck. "Don't rush home on our account."

He thought that was pretty good advice.

When he reached the Small Change ten minutes later, he found Theo just leaving. As before, Enrico drove the ranch truck. They stopped at the entrance to the driveway, each of them rolling down their window.

Theo winked at Gabe from his place in the passenger seat. "The antibiotics are in the main cattle barn supply room. Reese can show you. She's there now. I told her you were coming."

"I thought she didn't get home from work until five thirty."

"Appears she's anxious to see you."

Gabe's heart nearly exploded. She was waiting for him. Wanted to see him. Perhaps she regretted the other day and would give him another chance.

Please, he thought, one more small miracle.

"What are you waiting for?" Theo demanded, pretending impatience. "Get a move on."

The last thing Gabe heard as he rolled up his window was the older man's belly laugh.

Gabe drove straight to the main cattle barn, a giant structure about a half mile from the two-story ranch house. The supply room was at the south end. He took the corner too fast, causing the truck's brakes to squeal and the tires to cut wide grooves in the still-damp ground.

Reese burst from the supply room door and came to a sudden stop.

She wore a long, slim-fitting trench coat over something short. A skirt, maybe, or a dress. Gabe didn't care. All that mattered was he got a nice view of her legs. Shapely, smooth and bare. Was she nuts? It was cold outside. She must have been in a hurry to see him. No less of a hurry than he was in to see her.

He wrenched open his door and jumped out of the truck. She didn't move. Had Theo exaggerated in order to orchestrate a reconciliation? Rather than run to her, as was his first inclination, he proceeded slowly.

"I saw your dad as he was leaving. He said you'd show me where the antibiotics are stored."

Reese gestured at the supply room. "Sure."

He closed the distance between them and would have taken her hand if she didn't abruptly turn and lead him through the door.

The supply room was large, but crowded. Half of the available space was taken up by shelving units, the other half by cabinets, crates and trunks of varying sizes. Gabe spotted an old refrigerator in the corner that probably contained the antibiotics. This time, he led the way, down the narrow aisle and between the racks. Reese followed closely.

Rather than grab bottles, Gabe spun, coming face-to-face with her. His plan all along.

"Cole sold his roping horses."

"He did?"

"Now we can buy more hay and inseminate the cows."

"Wow. I'm surprised."

"That makes two of us." Gabe reminded himself to breathe. She was so close. Within touching distance. "We're going to survive the red nose outbreak and get the ranch out of debt."

"I believe you."

She wasn't making this easy for him. If he wanted her, he should make the effort. Maybe she knew that and was waiting.

Gabe had no intention of disappointing her. "I'm sorry, Reese. I was wrong."

"About what?"

She truly wasn't going to make this easy.

"Where to start?"

"Start with what's most important." Her warm, tender gaze melted the last of his doubts.

"I've been an idiot."

"It's not too late to change."

"You're what's most important. I shouldn't have let you go. What we have, what we could have, is incredibly special. The hell with you being the trustee or me not inheriting the entire ranch. None of that matters more than us."

She tilted her head appealingly. "Go on."

He drew her close. "I'd like to give us a try."

"There's still my job."

"I don't suppose you could quit." He squeezed her shoulders, wanting to kiss her, but waiting.

"No. But I could speak to Walt. I don't think this situation has come up at the bank before, but there has to be a workable compromise. If you and your brothers are in agreement, Walt could take over for me."

"If we're in agreement, you could stay on."

"Would Josh and Cole?" Hope blazed in her eyes.

"They like you."

"What about you?"

He hauled her against him, reveling in the feel of her soft, lush curves beneath her coat. Lowering his head, he brought his mouth to hers. "You know how I feel."

"Say it, Gabe."

"I fell in love with you that day in the mountains when I saw you trying to rescue your father's horse. I figured any woman crazy enough to think she could lift a thousand-pound horse by herself was crazy enough to love me back."

"You were right," she said and raised her lips to his.

Gabe lost himself in the wonder of Reese's kiss.

She was the one he'd been waiting for, the one worth fighting for, the one he could, and would, spend the rest of his life with. After today, and all the things he'd seen, nothing was impossible.

Epilogue

Christmas Day

Gabe couldn't remember seeing this many people gathered around the dining room table for Christmas dinner. The tradition of limiting the holiday meal to immediate family and friends was over. There were so many people they had had to set up an extra table.

In addition to Gabe's brothers, his mother and his *tio* Lorenzo, Cara was there with her mother and stepfather. Violet had also been invited, as well as the McGraws. *All* of the McGraws. Reese, naturally, her father and Aunt Louise, along with Reese's cousin

Megan, her husband and—this was really incredible—Celia.

During one of their many moments alone over the past few days, Reese had told Gabe that, rather than wait until spring break, Celia had asked to come for Christmas. Reese had mustered up her courage and told her father about Celia, only to learn he'd known all along and couldn't wait to meet his granddaughter.

After that, the pieces had fallen into place. Celia's parents were able to wrangle three airline tickets, and they'd arrived yesterday for a week-long visit. Gabe had been honored and touched to be included in the family reunion. It was a moment he'd remember all his life.

As was this special holiday. He and his brothers still had a long way to go in repairing their relationship. Years of animosity didn't disappear overnight. And the ranch remained at financial risk, though no more steer had come down with red nose. There were bumps in the road ahead for Gabe and Reese, as well, one being her father's illness. Yet with all that, the future looked brighter than it had for a long, long time. Since before his father had become ill.

"Mommy," Celia asked Megan in a bright

voice, "can I go riding tomorrow? Reese invited me."

"You're welcome to come with us," Reese added.

By us, she meant her and Gabe. He'd thought the idea was a good one when she'd mentioned it earlier.

"None of us have ridden much," Megan said, a bit dubiously.

"We have plenty of horses for beginners," Gabe said. "We promise to take it slow."

"All right." Megan smiled.

"Yippee." Celia nearly spilled her milk in her excitement. "Can Grandpa come, too?" She turned to Theo.

"I'll watch." He stroked her hair, his face that of a man ten years younger. Meeting his granddaughter was responsible.

Beneath the table, Gabe felt Reese's hand clasp his. He didn't have to look at her to know she was deeply moved.

He squeezed her fingers in return.

"Here's to our many blessings." His mother raised her glass in a toast, which everyone readily joined in. "And to a happy, prosperous New Year."

When Gabe clinked glasses with Reese's,

their eyes met. He couldn't say it at the table, but he tried to convey what was in his heart.

She must have understood, for she mouthed, "I love you."

The two of them had a chance at a future together, one of their own making. For Gabe, it included him and Reese and their brand-new combined family. The possibilities were endless.

Had his father known all along this would happen? Gabe liked to think so, and that he approved.

As if in answer, the musical Christmas tree began to play.

* * * * *

Get 4 FREE REWARDS!

We'll send you 2 FREE Books plus 2 FREE Mystery Gifts.

Harlequin Romance Larger-Print books will immerse you in emotion and intimacy simmering in international locales— experience the rush of falling in love!

FREE Value Over $20

Get 4 FREE REWARDS!

We'll send you 2 FREE Books plus 2 FREE Mystery Gifts.

FREE Value Over **$20**

Both the **Romance** and **Suspense** collections feature compelling novels written by many of today's bestselling authors.